Praise for
The Seductive Lady Vanessa of Manhattanshire

"Kaufman has written a witty and utterly original take on the
Don Quixote story—charming and unexpected."
— Miranda Heller, author of *NYT* bestseller
The Paper Palace

"Mad times call for mad literature. Seth Kaufman's zany and
hilarious re-interpretation of the *Don Quixote* legend, via a
delusional, middle-aged, romance novel junkie on the Upper
West Side, lives up to the challenge. Also, it has a happy
ending! Insofar as the novel otherwise defies description, I
strongly recommend you read it yourself."
— Lucinda Rosenfeld, author of *Class*

"*The Seductive Lady Vanessa* is tailor-made for all book addicts
seeking fun, adventure, and laughter. But romance fans
will find themselves particularly smitten as Lady Vee and
her Brooklyn-born lady-in-waiting caper through modern
Manhattan(shire) looking for love in all the wrong places.
Like its forerunners *Don Quixote* and *Pride and Prejudice*, the
book smuggles in deep human issues amid the antics: addiction in sneaky modern forms, loneliness amid vast crowds, and
acceptance of self as a bridge to freedom. This is a wonderful,
sharp, and laugh-out-loud work that takes a kind-eyed look at
the risks, struggles, and rewards of wanting a little love now."
— Robin McLean, author of *Pity the Beast*

"In *The Seductive Lady Vanessa of Manhattanshire*, Seth Kaufman not only brings Don Quixote's obsession with chivalric romances into the 21st century through the hilarious Manhattanite Lady Vee's mad passion for romance novels, but he also updates Cervantes's narrator Cide Hamete Benengeli through the suspenseful story of the Egyptian Aisha Benengeli, this novel's 'author.' A fit successor to the many works of wit and satire that have followed the path of *Don Quixote de la Mancha*, Kaufman's novel will satisfy readers seeking both Cervantes's metafictional play and ironic jabs at self-fashioning as well as Jane Austen's gentle satire of the business of romance."

—RACHEL SCHMIDT, author of *Forms of Modernity: Don Quixote and Modern Theories of the Novel*

THE
SEDUCTIVE
LADY
VANESSA
OF
MANHATTANSHIRE

A NOVEL

SETH KAUFMAN

Post Hill
PRESS

A POST HILL PRESS BOOK
ISBN: 978-1-63758-362-3
ISBN (eBook): 978-1-63758-363-0

The Seductive Lady Vanessa of Manhattanshire:
A Novel
© 2022 by Seth Kaufman
All Rights Reserved

Post Hill Press
New York • Nashville
posthillpress.com

Published in the United States of America
1 2 3 4 5 6 7 8 9 10

CONTENTS

TRANSLATOR'S NOTE #1

As a well-known Arabic scholar, I often receive requests to translate rare and challenging texts into English. But no assignment has ever left me as disturbed and perplexed as the strange tale I share with you now. It arrived in my mailbox, postmarked from Cairo, on March 3, 2019.

This is the correspondence that accompanied the manuscript:

Dear Ms. Noor,

The enclosed pages were inadvertently purchased in a shop in Cairo's Khan el-Khalili souk. Ali Mohammed, an illiterate trader with exceptionally large teeth, was hawking a large brown Yves Saint Laurent handbag festooned with the designer's initials. He informed me he had purchased it from a man who claimed that his sister-in-law's brother's wife's cousin's cousin had worked in a hotel and was given the bag by an Egyptian-American woman. For a reason she did not reveal, the hotel worker was very distressed and asked her relatives to get rid of this exceptionally well-designed brown carryall. That was all he could tell me. I bought the item from the vendor and later discovered the manuscript inside. My wife got the bag and I, in turn, got a headache trying to make sense of the strange story recounted in the pages, which I am now forwarding to you. I consider myself a modern man, but much of the story, written by someone named Aisha Benengeli, seems incomprehensible to me. Vertical chariot? Five Alarm Hothouse? What are these things? I soon gave up reading. Perhaps a gifted scholar such as yourself, who understands the Arabic language along with the unfathomable mysteries of American culture, will be able to make sense of this story.

Sincerely,
Sadeki Salah

I began at once to examine the manuscript Sadeki Salah had enclosed. I read deep into the night, transfixed, confused and shocked by a tale so bizarre, so comical, and yet so tragic that it stands far apart from all the other works I have encountered in my many decades as a translator of Arabic texts—including the beloved The False and Fallen Pharaoh of Luxor and His Army of Magical Asps *by Faisal Bin Mohammed, and the classic of early Egyptian erotica* Midnight at the Oasis: 101 Forbidden Tales of the Karnak Gardens.

It is every translator's task not only to render the author's words comprehensible in a different language but also to understand the goals, intent, and deeper themes of the author and convey them with a sort of invisible clarity.

In the case of The Seductive Lady Vanessa of Manhattanshire: A Novel *and its mysterious author, Aisha Benengeli, I had only the raw Arabic text to serve as my guide. I believe I have captured the tone and complex vision of the enigmatic and, as you will see, troubled Ms. Benengeli. Her creation, Lady Vanessa, is a confounding char-*

acter. But I have come to admire Lady Vee's spirit, madness, and mission, as well as the vision of her creator, who, as the story progresses, also shares her own strange tale.

At the risk of stating the obvious, I hope I have rendered the vision of Ms. Benengeli with the accuracy she deserves and that readers will share my amazement, delight, concern, and admiration for both the author and her singular heroine.

Oona Noor
Manhattan, NY
September 23, 2019

CHAPTER 1

In which Lady Vanessa loses her senses, accosts a plumber, and receives an unwanted literary cleansing

When Maxine More started speaking in a faux English accent, announced she was "technically a virgin," and declared the only name she would answer to was Lady Vanessa of Manhattanshire, her daughter Emma decided to go uptown and pay her mother a visit.

Emma's mission of mercy was already late in coming. Two weeks earlier, after resigning from her job as a kindergarten teacher, Maxine had begun to fully transform herself into Lady Vanessa.

She discovered an enormous circular lampshade lying discarded in her building's basement and had a vision. In a dangerous fever of industry, Her Ladyship stripped off the lampshade's dusty canvas covering, stitched two tablecloths together, and affixed them to the wire frame.

The result was a horrendous, ill-fitting creation—green and black gingham on one side and pink with white floral accents on the other—that Lady Vanessa deemed "a farthingale," or hoop skirt. Other than the eyesore color scheme and the shoddy needlework, the chief problem with Lady Vanessa's getup was the fact that the foundational lampshade wire was circular and lacked the precise shaping—flat at the front, wide at the side, and bulbous at the back—to assure the vast acreage of the dress would swell and rise in her wake, as such dresses are meant to do.

Instead, Lady Vanessa stood marooned in the middle of her abominable handiwork. The skirt swelled in a circular fashion around her hips, leaving the remainder of her unwired drapes flapping around her legs, for the lampshade frame was little more than a sturdy, too-large chassis and failed, as true hoop skirts do, to accentuate the posterior with wire support all the way down to the floor.

As for her face, Lady Vanessa was a firm believer that less makeup is not more for women of a certain age. Although youth might be served with only a faint powder, a mild shade of lipstick, or a dab of blush to bring out the rosiness of cheeks, she did not believe such restraint would work for her forty-eight-year-old face. In her hands, a simple compact became a weapon of self-destruction. Maxine's bright blue eyes, dark hair, prominent nose, and full-lipped mouth were rather fetching and needed no camouflage, but they were obliterated by her transformation into Lady Vanessa.

Taking a page out of Daphne Warrenspunk's *The Widow's Revenge* and the wisdom of its heroine, Melanie Raft—a chaste, kind cosmetologist whose late movie-producer husband was blackmailed into leaving his entire estate to the children of his first wife—Lady Vanessa made Melanie's observation that "lips are the ultimate lure of love" into the first commandment of personal grooming.

She was never without a rouged mouth. And, again thanks to heartbroken, desperate Melanie, who swore by bright magentas, impassioned cherries, and scandalous scarlets, Lady Vanessa favored loud, glistening lipstick.

But her fiery crimson mouth was just the beginning of her misguided transformation. She applied moisturizer to her cheeks, dried and powdered them, and added a thick layer of blush. She plucked and buffed her eyebrows and caked her naked lashes heavily with mascara. In her mind—and in the mind of fictional Melanie, who triumphantly rose above her calamitous fate to find a perfect mate of body and soul in Lyle Sanderson, her dead husband's kindhearted cameraman—the contrast between the various red shades and the darkening of the eyes enhanced the riot of tonal beauty.

In Lady Vanessa's hands, however, the makeup resulted only in visual chaos. The lipstick often wound up smeared on her teeth so that her smile resembled an unrepentant cannibal's grin. The blush lent her face a clownish mien. And her dark zombie eyes were more alarming than alluring.

The unsettling sight of Lady Vanessa brazenly strolling Broadway's crowded sidewalks was something passersby would not soon forget. Some thought she looked like a walking, anthropomorphized junk shop. Others wondered if she was some kind of street performer or bizarre master clown. Discerning pedestrians looked at Lady Vanessa and saw madness, while the more empathetic gazed at her face and saw tragedy.

Although most streetwise citizens gave Lady Vanessa a wide berth as she proudly strutted her mangled Georgian look—her hoop skirt dragging along the filthy pavement, her face a riot of color—more than one well-meaning pedestrian approached her, motivated by sympathy and concern.

"Oh my god! Who did that to you?" said a shocked young woman sporting a buzzcut and a "Be the Change!" T-shirt. "I hope he's in jail!"

"Excuse me?" said a perplexed Lady Vanessa.

"Do you have a place to go? I volunteer at a women's shelter."

"My good woman, I cannot fathom a word of your meaning!" declared Lady Vanessa. "I am *Lady* Vanessa of Manhattanshire, and I have resided in this precinct for nearly three decades!"

"Oh. I thought—"

"I have no idea what you thought. But it is customary to curtsy before those with the status of a ladyship. But I see you are like my daughter: utterly clueless when it comes to comportment."

"Sorry! My bad," said the good Samaritan, rolling her eyes. "Have a nice day."

This was far from the only encounter provoked by Lady Vanessa's unique ensemble.

On various promenades, other well-meaning men and women—including a pastor and a social worker—also asked if Lady Vanessa needed help, suspecting the racoon-eyed results of the strangely dressed woman's cosmetological efforts were masking a beating.

"Excuse me, ma'am," said the social worker. "Can I give you a number to call if you are having relationship problems? Or have been assaulted?"

These encounters always left Lady Vanessa confused. "I've been divorced for well over a decade!" she declared to the misguided do-gooders. "The only assault I have ever endured is the one taking place right now!"

On the day her daughter Emma arrived at her mother's West End Avenue apartment, the self-described "Lady of the Manor" was about to set out for a "secret assignation."

"That's redundant, Mom. Assignations are always secret. And you look ridiculous."

Lady Vanessa was decked out in a new ensemble, the centerpiece of which was a ragged hoop skirt she'd found at a Thespians of Broadway rummage sale. As Emma gazed at her mother's ratty dress, the rouge on her cheeks, the bonnet on her head, and parasol in her hand, she thought this so-called "Lady" looked like a fallen woman at a Renaissance fair who had imbibed too much Ye Olde Ale.

"You're just jealous," murmured Lady Vanessa. "Your aerodynamic figure is no match for the allure of my curves and comeliness."

Emma, a slender young woman with jet-black hair and oversized glasses that made her seem smaller than she was, shook her head in disbelief and tried to make sense of her mother's disturbing condition.

Her mother was obsessed with what she sometimes referred to as "my stories," "my inspirations," or "my touchstones."

These were books wherein hearts heave or cleave—and often do both—before finally melting and melding with a perfect man, but only after overcoming such suitably dramatic obstacles as: evil sisters; vicious stepmothers; lascivious step-fathers; stolen inheritances and titles; conniving, gold-digging ex-wives; family cruelties; crippling illnesses; bodily injury; penury; and all other manner of personal devastation.

Although the books varied in subject, milieu, and lustiness, Emma knew them not as "my touchstones," in her mother's parlance, but as the bodice-ripping romances they were.

She also understood—thanks to her mother's enraptured and endless recounting of the plotlines—that these books all dealt with the unshakable longings of hearts and loins and the heroine's brave quest to live in blissful union with the perfect mate.

The men in these books were vastly different from those Lady Vanessa had encountered in her once-fledgling but now completely dormant dating life. Indeed, the male species populating the pages of these romances did not arrive at the door with a twelve-pack of beer and a plan to watch six hours of football on TV. Nor did they call from a bar at one thirty in the morning to ask if "you're in the mood for a visit" or inquire, "What are you wearing?" in slurred voices. And if they were delayed in their arrival for a date, it was not due to a mishap on the subway or "extra innings" or an alleged "son-of-a-bitch boss"—it was because they were   closing a multibillion-dollar business deal, solving a kidnapping, or stricken with a case of sudden amnesia. That's assuming they weren't helping a runaway bride free herself from a black-hearted villain, or another woman was conspiring to win his attention and they were too well-mannered to dismiss the cunning bitch.

Or, just as likely, they were avenging a grievous wrong—a stolen inheritance, a callous power play, a blood libel against the family, responding to a five-alarm fire with children in dire need of rescue, or helping save an elderly aunt's crumbling farm from a murderous thief—or any of the various and sundry daily quandaries someone such as a pirate, billionaire, or secret son of a king might find himself involved in.

These unique characters were "real men" to Lady Vanessa, ideal specimens who encompassed a perfectly calibrated combination of masculine beauty, elegant manners, royal comportment, testosterone-driven courage, and heroic inclinations that were sometimes, almost tragically, mistaken as criminal behavior.

Oh, there were other types, too, and Lady Vanessa had studied them all. Handsome and hunky but all-suffering; buff and blond but hurt and victimized; black haired with piercing blue eyes but haunted by dark secrets, tragic lost loves, enforced betrothals, or stolen fortunes; impossibly decent but cursed by fate's unfathomable injustices.

There were also the tattooed and grease-stained bikers, driven from their beloved homesteads by jealous and greedy siblings; billionaire businessmen lonely for understanding; secret agents with a mistake that haunted them—all soul-wounded, God-fearing men who would never take advantage of a lady, no matter how much that lady might be ready for an advantage to be taken.

And speaking of advantage being taken, there was one other variant of the species: rogues. These were men of unbridled passion and unrivaled good looks and charm who refused to let the subterranean passions of a woman lie dormant. A rogue's conquest would, however, often be his undoing. While bedding the object of his affection, an unsurpassed sexual encounter would transpire and a rogue would find himself transformed by the loving and lusty response of the woman he had seduced and, having tasted true love's nectar, find himself unable to live without it. A modern-day, true drop-your-knickers rogue was rare, as Emma understood it, but might prove to be a true ticket to happiness.

"Mom," said Emma, "you're from New Jersey. Your name is Maxine. You live on the Upper West Side. You're forty-eight, and if you're a virgin, well then, I guess I must be Jesus. Also, I'm almost twenty-two, which means the child support payments from Dad—which I never get anyway—are going to stop pretty soon. And you quit your job. So let's try to get back to reality, okay?"

"Balderdash and poppycock, Emma," declared Lady Vanessa. "I said 'technically' because I have never truly given my heart to my perfect soulmate. I remain a *lady* with my heart intact and I shall comport myself as such. Now allow me to summon the vertical chariot so I may go meet the duke, earl, billionaire, fireman, or cowboy of my destiny."

"Maria!" Emma called, hoping her mother's twice-a-week cleaning woman was there. "Maria! Are you here?"

"I have given Maria the day off. What I do with my staff is my business. I'm sure you are just after my suitors, anyway, you vile temptress."

"Mom! I've *got* a boyfriend, remember? *Nick?*"

Lady Vanessa stepped out of her apartment, walked toward the elevator, and then turned to her daughter. "Nick? The boy who dallies with computers?"

"Yes. The guy I've been dating for eighteen months!"

"After your virtue, no doubt, on the slim chance you still have it."

"Mom!"

The elevator door opened. A man wearing coveralls stepped out. The logo on his chest pocket identified him as an employee of Grey's Plumbing. He was, in truth, an uninspiring figure. His sparse, wildly sprouting hair was in need of a barber, his posture in need of alignment, his stature in need of height, his girth in need of reduction, and his pants, as anyone who witnessed him kneeling on the job would see, greatly in need of a belt.

But Lady Vanessa gazed at the plumber, glimpsed the company name on his shirt, and saw an entirely different man.

"*Christian,*" she gasped. "I see you have finally come to your senses and left that tramp Anastasia. I know we—"

"I'm here for apartment Twelve C."

"Oh, no! I live in Twelve F, silly man! Do come in." She grabbed his arm and, noticing his bag of plumber tools, said, "Oh, you've brought your wicked bag of restraints! How presumptuous! You know I am a woman of great beauty and decorum."

The plumber sent a look of appeal to Emma, who was paralyzed with embarrassment, and said, "I'm pretty sure the work order said Twelve C. Clogged pipes?"

"I can assure you that no one who has ever felt the gift of my passion has complained of clogged pipes," said Lady Vanessa. "Now, my handsome multimillionaire, come inside and woo me."

The plumber stopped and turned again to Emma, who was wondering if she should ask her mother if her pipe cleaning reference obliterated any claims to virginity.

"Am I getting filmed?" he asked. "You know, punked or catfished? Like that old show my grandma watched? *Candid Camera?*"

"Mom! Please leave this man alone. He's come to fix the pipes in Mr. Miller's apartment."

"Christian Grey, is this one of your power trips? Taunting me? Teasing me? Well, it's working, but I shall turn the tables on you, for my womanly presence is a powerful aphrodisiac widely known to billionaire industrialists, firemen, and soldiers in Manhattanshire and beyond, as well as men whose first loves died tragic deaths and whose hearts are wounded beyond any hope of repair!"

And with that declaration, Lady Vanessa slapped the bewildered plumber in the face.

"Jesus, Mom!"

"Lady, are you fucking nuts?"

"That is for ignoring me and spending time with that little harlot Anastasia. Consider yourself lucky that none of my hulking, be-muscled construction worker or engine company woo-ers are around to defend my honor."

By this time, Arlene Gold, the retired librarian who lived in apartment 12E and had curly, salt-and-pepper hair and a perpetually earnest expression of concern on her face, and Natalie Ringer, the upbeat waitress with strawberry-blonde hair and an extensive collection of track suits in 12A, had come out to the hallway.

"What's going on? Everything all right?" asked Arlene.

"This friggin' nutjob just slapped me in the face for no reason," said the plumber.

"Are you okay?" said Natalie.

"Yeah, I'm fine. But she's outta her mind," said the plumber, nodding toward Maxine.

"My mother has gone a little off the deep end," cried Emma. "I'm so sorry, sir."

The two neighbors approached Maxine.

"Let's go inside and have a cup of tea, Maxine," said Arlene, putting her hand on her distraught neighbor's arm.

"Vassals! Serfs! Enemies of true love! Take your hands off me! I am Lady Vanessa, known far and wide as the beautiful maiden of Manhattanshire."

"Please, Mom," said Emma, pulling her mother back into the apartment. She called out to the plumber. "I'm so sorry, sir. She's really not well."

"Of course I'm well. It is Mr. Grey who requires a lady's help!"

"My name is Ernie Murphy, you freaking crazy person!"

Mr. Miller, the tall, unfailingly polite and smiling inhabitant of 12C, who always wore a tweed blazer—even, apparently, while relaxing in his own home—suddenly opened his apartment door.

"Hello!" he boomed. "Did a plumber come—"

"Mr. Miller?" said Ernie Murphy.

"Yes! Ah, there you are! Come in, come in. Is everything alright?"

"Not really, but I'll survive," said the plumber, nodding at Lady Vanessa while turning his forefinger in circles at the side of his head.

"Oh," said Mr. Miller, flashing a look of confusion.

"Maxine mistook him for someone else, Mr. Miller. She's not herself," explained Natalie, before heading into Maxine's apartment.

Arlene and Natalie helped Emma usher Lady Vanessa into her bedroom. They waited with Lady Vanessa while Emma made a cup of chamomile tea spiked with Ambien. They helped Lady Vanessa disrobe, a process that was quite an ordeal given her garters, girdle, bustier, camisole, hoop, stockings, and lacy unmentionables. Finally, after finishing her tea in a huff, Lady Vanessa's eyes began to close and she collapsed onto her bed.

"Are you alright?" Natalie asked Emma.

"I'm fine. But my mother has let her damn books get into her head."

"You mean the romances?"

"Exactly. Come and look."

Emma led them to the dining room, which no longer served its original purpose. The large table and a matching set of chairs in the middle of the room were covered with teetering stacks of well-worn paperbacks. Some of the covers of these books featured women in elaborate Georgian-era finery. Others depicted men and women clenched in various dramatic embraces. Still others featured the chiseled midriffs of muscular, bare-chested men. The bookcases that lined the walls were also stuffed, their shelves sagging under the weight of romances wedged into every available inch of space.

"Oh my," murmured Arlene with a sense of horror and admiration. "This is impressive."

"Impressive? These books have destroyed her life!" said Emma.

"Are they all romances?"

"Yes. She reads them nonstop, muttering and moaning all the way through. And when she's not reading, she has conversations with unseen lovers and tries to introduce me to these apparitions! Or worse, she accuses me of trying to steal them away from her. She needs serious help."

"Maybe you should call her doctor," said Arlene. "Or a psychiatrist."

"She refuses to see anyone but her dermatologist and her dentist."

"Oh dear."

"We should start by getting rid of these books," Emma said. "I'm sick of them."

"Why don't you see if her doctor will make a house call today?" asked Natalie. "I know it's a long shot, but give it a try. Arlene and I will start going through this collection and root out the worst offenders. Right, Arlene?"

"Sure. I was a librarian for thirty years. Weeding out books comes with the territory. We always had to make room on the shelves for new books."

"No! No more books, please God!" said Emma, heading toward the phone in the kitchen.

The two neighbors turned to survey the room and realized the daunting task ahead of them.

"Where do we start?" wondered Natalie.

"Here!" Arlene Gold plucked a book off the shelf. "Damn that Tabitha Hartland. She has a lot to answer for. All those demure damsels and those dreadful circular covers that look as if they were drawn on porcelain plates. She shall be the first to burn."

"No, certainly that honor goes to this," said Natalie Ringer, holding up a copy of *Diamond Hard* by Sonia Horn. "This carnal catalog is nothing more than porn dressed in love's clothing."

"True, but that was nothing compared to her second effort, *Diamond in the Buff.* Grab that too! It was a smut fest with little else to recommend it."

"Well, Salome did help cure Darryl's low blood pressure."

"And I suppose she stopped Aunt Agatha marrying that cad who was only after her money."

"Still, that scene in the bathroom was totally inappropriate."

They tossed all three books to the floor.

"Now," said Arlene Gold, "it seems to me that Donna Reeves's *Five Alarm Hothouse* has much to answer for."

"I never heard of it. My uncle is a fireman."

"Did he look like this?" Arlene Gold held up a book. On the cover, a swarthy, shirtless man with rippling six-pack abs wrapped a gorgeous blonde in his arms.

Natalie Ringer took the book, studied it, and said, "Maybe eighty or ninety pounds ago."

"My point exactly. Here. She has the entire series: *Red, Hot, and Brave, Brave & Buff, Brave & Built, Burning Desires, The Company Man, Five Alarm Hothouse to the Rescue, Conflagrations & Palpitations*, and the absolutely filthy *Fire Pole.*"

They flung these overheated odes to the bravest onto the floor as well.

"Now look. An entire bookcase devoted to Nanette Meyer," huffed Natalie Ringer.

"I admit that of all the raconteurs of romance, Meyer has her strong points."

"The Harmony series?"

"Yes! Her glorious rendering of civil society, the clothes, the parties, the manners. I must confess a weak spot."

"But look what they've done to Lady Vanessa. I mean, Maxine. They've cast a spell on her and ruined her mind!"

"True, but at least they're devoted to ladies and not the strumpets that populate, say, *Consent and Control* or *Whip Smart* or *The Pound & The Fury.*"

"Is that the one about Jessica Hume, the impoverished, kind, and curvaceous woman who runs a rescue shelter, and the handsome, irreparably damaged dog walker, Brett Ravelle, who doesn't know he's been left a fortune by an old client?"

"Yes, though I only skimmed it."

"I'm younger than you, Arlene. And frankly, those more modern books get my heart beating a bit faster than Meyer's *Harmony's Choice.* But no matter our different tastes, the fact remains: these books seem to have propelled poor Maxine into a psychosis."

Arlene Gold sighed. "You're right, Natalie."

"How's it going?" Emma returned to the room.

"Very well. But we're going to need some empty boxes to dispose of this overheated garbage."

"I'm way ahead of you," Emma said, brandishing a box of large garbage bags. "Anything else?"

"No," said Natalie Ringer, "unless you want to help us tackle Jane Austen."

"We cannot, or rather, *I* cannot, as a former librarian, toss out Jane," said Arlene.

"But she is the source, the urtext, the poisoned root of what afflicts Emma's mother."

"Oh, yes! Please," said Emma. "Throw them out! If I hear one more mention of that damned Mr. Darcy, I'll throw myself out with them."

"I say," said Natalie, "I find myself talking in a rather odd manner these last few moments."

"Yes. Just touching an Austen book can make a woman from Hoboken put on airs and graces; look at my mom."

"Into the bag, quick!"

"Yes! All of it, please!" urged Emma.

They came to another shelf.

"Ooh, look at this," said Arlene Gold.

"Oh yes, love poetry," said Emma. "Get rid of it!"

"But the language is so lovely," said the former librarian.

"Sure, but who talks like that?" asked Natalie.

"My mother's imaginary suitors," said Emma. "They have the gift of the gab, seducing her with cloying couplets she takes personally. As if they're about her beauty and virtue. About how only she understands them and how her looks rival Helen of Troy, which practically forces men to write stanzas pledging their undying allegiance. It's awful."

"I disagree again," said Arlene, "but I see I'm outvoted."

And so away went *Love Poems, More Love Poems, Love Poems for Lovers, Odes of the Heart, Sonnets of Passion,* and *1001 Poems for Wooing, Winning and Sinning.*

The bag was now full. Emma flapped open a new one. "We need to speed things up," she said. "My mother's sleep is agitated, even with Ambien."

"Did you get through to the doctor?"

"I left a message."

Now Emma opened the dining room window, which looked down at the alleyway at the side of the building, hoisted the bag to the sill, and pushed it out the window.

"What about that unholy trinity *Fifty Shades of Grey?*" said Arlene.

"Yes! I believe your mother mistook the plumber for the lusty lothario of that series," said Natalie.

"And for that they shall perish," said Arlene, tossing them into the new garbage bag.

"And don't forget the new series by Fiona Way. They've been sliced and diced into more books than you can imagine."

"What's this?" Arlene said, holding up *Rawhide Mountain.* "Why are there two hulking himbos on the cover?"

"What, you didn't have gay romances at your library?" asked Natalie.

"Not that I remember."

"My mother adores cowboys of all predilections, love being love," said Emma.

"Of course. So is the entire Bareback Raiders series, um…?"

"Gay as *Brokeback Mountain,*" Emma said, opening the bag wider. "But we must not discriminate. Everything must go!"

⊱⋛⋋𝒳⋌⋚⊰

Emma stayed with her mother for a few days. Maxine, exhausted by the heart-stopping run-in with her imaginary Christian Grey and the Ambien, was calm and contrite. Her doctor, worried about overmedicating, advised counseling, chamomile tea, and exercise, all of which Maxine refused.

But Maxine—or Lady Vanessa, as she continued to think of herself—realized Emma was alarmed by her behavior. It was clear her daughter intended to remain in the apartment until she was convinced her mom had stabilized.

To that end, Maxine eliminated any discussion of romance, sex, or her eternal goal of finding a handsome, decent soulmate with a large estate. Privately, she seethed over Emma throwing out half of her library. This was a betrayal of the highest order to Lady Vanessa. But except for a few pointed barbs directed at her daughter, she refused to reveal the depth of her wound, consoling herself with the reality that books could be replaced. She talked about food, about how New York was changing, about the news, and about Emma's job and boyfriend. She also dug up an old murder mystery that she carried around the apartment, acting spellbound by its pages.

In her discussions with Emma, Maxine refrained from referring to herself as Lady Vanessa and answered to Maxine or Mom. Inwardly, this caused her great pain, for in her heart and mind she remained Lady Vanessa, a woman with a vast knowledge of romance and comportment who, beneath a cool and demure demeanor, burned with deep, dark passions that roiled her very soul.

After a week of good behavior, Lady Vanessa realized her daughter was not about to leave any time soon, despite paying a small fortune for her room in a dismal, overpriced railroad apartment in Brooklyn.

"It's cool, Mom," Emma said, explaining that her boy-friend Nick was a coder who made a lot of money and would help pay her rent. "Anyway, I want to make sure you get settled into therapy like Dr. Vendela suggested."

This, however, was not cool with Lady Vanessa.

"Darling Emma, I understand your concern for me, and frankly, I'm touched. But you have a life of your own. Would it put your mind at rest if we hired someone to visit with me every day or every other day? Maria has a cousin named Magdalena."

"I thought Maria was your 'lady-in-waiting,'" Emma scoffed.

"Don't be ridiculous. She's been our cleaning lady for your entire life. But she's going to the Dominican Republic on what may be a permanent vacation."

"She's retiring?"

"She isn't sure. But that's why she mentioned her cousin Magdalena, who is supposed to be a wonderful young woman."

"Do you have her number? Can I talk to her?"

"Sure. I'll get it from Maria."

"If we get you in therapy and this woman can clean and look in on you, then I'll go back to Brooklyn."

"Well, I certainly hope you'll come check on your old mother," Lady Vanessa lied.

"Count on it!"

⚜

And so, while Emma grew more confident that her mother was improving, Lady Vanessa resolved to find a kindred spirit, a lesser beauty who might understand the all-consuming search for destiny, for romance, for the perfect man, and who would know that taking the position of lady-in-waiting for a soon-to-be duchess or princess would increase her own likelihood of meeting a worthy gentleman, a man determined to make wild but respectful love to such a good, wholesome, dedicated servant. Yes, she needed a wing woman, as it were, to accompany her in her quest for a perfect and passionate mate.

When Maria's cousin showed up, Lady Vanessa had to suppress her giddiness. Magdalena Cruz was perfect. She was young, tall, hefty, and blonde, with a titanic bosom.

Although she was not particularly pretty, her face marred by thick, heavy features, she had an outgoing manner and seemed unabashed. When Lady Vanessa asked Magdalena if she had "any extracurricular passions," she said, "You mean like sports or a boyfriend? Nah. I mean, around my way guys are just out for hookups. I like to watch reality TV, yo. Like *16 and Pregnant.*"

Lady Vanessa concluded that although Magdalena was a little rough around the edges, those edges could be smoothed. And anyway, on the streets of New York, which were said to be teeming with handsome, rich alpha males but often seemed desolate and filled with riffraff, having an edge could be useful.

Emma wasn't quite sure how her mother would bond with a nineteen-year-old high school graduate from Sunset Park, Brooklyn, but she was thrilled that her mother seemed to like Magdalena. She offered the teenager twelve dollars an hour for four to six hours a day and said she wanted Magdalena to call her twice a week with updates.

"I'm all over that deal like beans on rice, yo," said Magdalena.

Emma moved back in with her boyfriend, and Lady Vanessa felt her heart lift. She would turn Magdalena into her confidante, her aide *d'amour*, her go-between, her shield, and her advocate. She would teach her how to dress, how to speak, how to comport herself, and how to lure the male species and tame them. Oh, this was going to be wonderful. This girl had no idea! As lady-in-waiting to the desirable Lady Vanessa of Manhattanshire, she would be the recipient of the trickle-down theory of riches and romance. Together, they would be the talk of the kingdom!

CHAPTER 2

In which Lady Vanessa finds her aide *d'amour,* explains Mr. Grey, rescues a prospect, and explores the voodoo of love

Despite her fervor to resume life as the Upper West Side's most eligible and elegant noble, Lady Vanessa knew she had to proceed with caution. She was aware that her meddling daughter Emma planned to monitor her behavior using Magdalena as a spy. The idea that her very own daughter was working to thwart the blossoming of love and happiness filled Lady Vanessa with fury. Indeed, the brazen purge of Lady Vanessa's unmatched library of romances—Emma and the wenches next door had thrown out nearly *half* her most precious books—was an unforgivable act. And when Lady Vanessa mourned the loss of her collection aloud, Emma had the nerve to say she had done it "for your own good."

Lady Vanessa could only attribute this behavior to Emma's father's genes. She had to; otherwise, she would never be able to forgive her daughter. Ever.

Lady Vanessa knew she had to counter Emma's scheming ways before she could broach the subject of transforming Magdalena into the most desirable lady-in-waiting in all of Manhattanshire. She needed to win over the giant teenager's allegiance and establish who, exactly, was in charge of her employment.

And so, on the Friday of Magdalena's first week of work, Lady Vanessa—who was still being called Ms. More by her new charge—brought out her checkbook. "What was the agreed-upon compensation for your services, Magdalena?"

"Oh no, Ms. More, Emma said she'd pay me."

"Nonsense! You work for me, and I shall pay you."

"But Emma said she'd do it. She said twelve dollars an hour."

"Let us make it fifteen, hmm?"

"If you're sure that's alright. I don't wanna cause no trouble."

"My dear girl, last week I was not feeling well. *I* suggested Emma call you. *She* was helping *me*. But I am a grown woman, and I—not my daughter—am completely in control of my life and my finances. I employed your cousin Maria for nearly twenty years. And I will pay you too. Now, I realize that Emma's overbearing behavior may have led you to believe otherwise, but I am in full command of my faculties. It is she, Emma, who wants to squelch my destiny, who does not want to see her own mother fulfilled with the true, kind, and wealthy lover all women deserve."

"Wow. She's stopping you from that? I had no idea, Ms. More."

"You may call me Lady Vanessa from henceforth, Magdalena. That is my preferred title, and one that Emma, in her vile jealousy, objects to."

"Lady Vanessa? That's mad fancy! By the way, Lady Vanessa, you can always call me Maggie, if you want. That's what I'm used to 'round my way in Brooklyn."

"Absolutely not! I shall do no such thing! Magdalena is a beautiful, sonorous name. It is perfectly befitting of a lady-in-waiting. Maggie is a fine name, too, of course. But it is truly no match for the sophistication and romance of Magdalena."

"Okay. I was just saying. I'm happy with it too."

"In fact, I was just thinking how grand it will be to introduce you as my lady-in-waiting Magdalena Stanislaw Cruz."

"Lady-in-waiting? Is that me?"

"Yes. If you choose to accept my offer. Normally, the position goes to a noble woman of lesser rank. But you seem so natural for the position—young, vivacious, and responsible—that I will make an exception."

"So I'm more than a cleaner and home aide?"

"Much, much more! Although the Mistress of Robes used to be the most important lady-in-waiting, these modern times have given the position more flexibility. You shall be my cleaning woman, my personal assistant, and, most importantly, my aide *d'amour*."

"Aide *d'amour*? Yo, I'm not sure about that. I only swing one way, Lady Vanessa. Not that I judge or anything."

"No, no, no, Magdalena! An aide *d'amour* is French for a love deputy, a go-between or, as I believe the phrase is used today, a wingwoman. Someone who helps bring about romance between a lady and a gentleman, ensuring a lady is at her most enticing and alluring."

"Ooh. Yeah, I do that with some of my girls back home. Like Yolanda? I introduced her to Eddie Biggs."

"Well, it is my sincere hope you will do that for me. And of course, it goes without saying that our relationship works both ways in the matter of finding a suitable partner. As a lady, I will come in contact with men of means who have their own staff of available men. And these best friends, chiefs of staff, and butlers, many of whom are handsome and well-off in their own right, may woo you."

"Really? Me?"

"Oh yes. It is well documented in Elsbeth Eversome's *The Servant Queen*, Katrina Covington's *The Best Best Man*, and Monique D'Oro's *Asking for a Friend*, that fetching ladies-in-waiting and other deserving underlings often find true, enduring, exceedingly passionate love with those employed by their betters. It is the way of the world, my girl."

"I can't believe it. This is like getting paid to go on Tinder, yo!"

"I have no idea what you are talking about, Magdalena. And we will have to address your verbal skills, comportment, dress, and make-up. But all in due time. Does this role, which I believe with all my soul that you were born to play, interest you?"

"Oh, yes, ma'am. I mean, Lady Vanessa. Sign me up. Ain't no men of means in Sunset Park, yo!"

"Good. I take that as an affirmative."

Although she now had an ally in Magdalena, Lady Vanessa of Manhattanshire was still not fully herself and not quite ready to resume her quest to find a worthy man. The scars left by her altercation with the plumber—a.k.a. untrustworthy cad Christian Grey—lingered for weeks. As she explained to her new lady-in-waiting, there were any number of reasons for the man's bizarre and callous disregard for the beauteous damsel before him.

"It is the nature of the alpha male to be a lone wolf and to resist giving his heart utterly and totally to one woman," Lady Vanessa said to a mystified yet attentive Magdalena.

"Numerous alpha males have twin brothers, however. And often these brothers clash, for a strong fraternal bond may present a point of vulnerability, which was the case in *Eden's Twin* by Saundra Garland. Or, conversely, the bond may feed the alphas' competitive and dominating nature. This was exactly the case with the O'Leary twins in *Mirror Images* by Blaze de la Croix. And for either of these reasons, the twins may be estranged."

"You're saying he wasn't Christian, but he was Christian's twin?" asked Magdalena, who hung on Her Ladyship's every word like the earnest student of a delusional lecturer, struggling to decode the complex, muddled logic and ever hopeful the confusion would give way to clarity.

Indeed, Magdalena wanted nothing more than for Lady Vanessa's assessments and pronouncements to be 100 percent correct, for Her Ladyship had assured her towering and earnest employee that a loyal, mesmerizingly handsome and dedicated man of unmatched decency and ardor awaited her, most likely working in service of the man who would eventually capture Lady Vanessa's body and soul.

"I am saying it is certainly one possibility, although I don't recall any mention of Christian having a twin," answered Lady Vanessa. "There are two other strong possibilities that cannot be discounted."

"What are they?"

"One involves the sinister machinations of the underworld. Surely you have read of the men who become bedeviled by ancient dazzlers and magicians such as the Legion of the Amulet, the Spectrum Brotherhood, or the Dark Knights of the Scarab. These men belong to another realm and have nothing better to do than export their eternal underworld misery to our realm and meddle in the lives of we mortals."

"Oh, you mean like vampires and *Twilight* and that creepy fucking shit?"

"Exactly. But please, Magdalena, I am a *lady*, and you are my lady-in-waiting. Such coarse language is simply not appropriate unless you are giving yourself over to the abandon of the ecstasy of the passion of true love with a kinky alpha male or ruffian biker."

"Sorry, Lady Vee. But that stuff creeps me out."

"Yes, battling the paranormal in the arena of love is no high tea with clotted cream and scones. Of that you may be certain. And you are not alone in your feelings of revulsion. But fear not, many of the denizens of the underworld desire to do good. They are trapped there, dreaming of release. It is their cursed rivals who, in the service of Beelzebub, surface to wreak havoc on the citizens of the Earth's crust. And that may be what has happened to Mr. Grey."

"But the ladies down the hall told me it wasn't him."

"What do those harlots and Delilahs know?" cried Lady Vanessa. "You injure me with their words!"

"No, their names are Arlene and—"

"I know their names, my dear Magdalena, but not their motives."

Lady Vanessa rose and began to dress for her morning promenade. But her mind was still wrapped up in her exchange with the plumber who disavowed her love. "There is one last possibility that those so-called neighbors have failed to consider. Amnesia!"

"Amnesia?"

"Yes, amnesia!"

"Who's she? Christian's other girlfriend?"

"No, Magdalena! No! Amnesia is the most tragic mental condition ever known to thwart the righteous destiny of two hearts merging. The poor man's memory has simply vanished, and he can't remember me and our passionate connection."

"Oh my God, that's so terrible," Magdalena said. The young woman wondered how this affliction might impact her. "Does that mean he would forget everybody, like his man-in-waiting or his bestie?"

"Often that is exactly the case, although a man-in-waiting, or bestie, as you put it, is more commonly known as a butler, guy Friday, knight, sidekick, or confidant. I've read stories where everything—knowledge of all prior relationships—has vanished: *Forever or Forgotten*, *Forget Her Not*, *The Muted Fire*, *The Unknown Earl*, and *Billionaire Hobo*. The heroes of these books all had their memory banks completely erased, so they didn't realize they were noblemen or rich alpha males or magnificently endowed firemen with vast inheritances."

"Damn, that's like losing your cell phone but a thousand times worse."

"Exactly. And I fear that is what may have happened with Christian."

"Is there a cure?"

"There are many, but it is hard to know which will be effective."

"*Dios mio, o boze!*" exclaimed Magdalena in both the Spanish and Polish of her parents.

"Do not despair, Magdalena, my dear," counseled Lady Vanessa of Manhattanshire. "First we must find him. And then we will rely on the power of true love to break the wretched spell."

⚬⚬⚬

Although Lady Vanessa talked a good game about the dismally out of shape man from Grey's Plumbing who was, in fact, named Ernie and not Christian, there was another gentleman who had caught her attention months earlier.

His name was Nelson Dodge, and he lived on the third floor of Lady Vanessa's building with a black poodle named Trixie. He was, in Lady Vanessa's eyes, a paragon of masculine beauty in its most appealing form: dark eyes, an olive complexion, just above average height, and small facial features that rendered him preternaturally and permanently "cute." He was also graced with kinky, curly dark hair so that he resembled his spunky poodle, a coincidence that Lady Vanessa cooed over whenever she spied the two together.

It is a truth universally acknowledged in New York City that a single, well-coiffed man in possession of a small dog named Trixie might telegraph certain alternative lifestyle choices and sexual preferences. But Lady Vanessa was utterly blind to these signals where Nelson Dodge was concerned.

Every journey in the vertical chariot, every trip to the building's mailroom or to the laundry facilities in the basement was viewed as a potential opportunity to glimpse the divine, well-muscled Nelson Dodge, who was always pleasant, well-mannered, good-humored, and seemed to truly relish discussing Lady Vanessa's hoop skirts and imitation pearls—never once indicating he knew they were fake—and who talked to Trixie as if the dog were a small child.

It was Nelson Dodge who Lady Vanessa hoped to impress as she and Magdalena set out one morning to visit a distant nail salon that was rumored to carry the most alluring, exotic, and intoxicating polishes.

"They have colors from Korea and China that you've never seen before," reported Magdalena. "Like panda black and lychee nut yellow. Colors that make men mad horny, yo!"

Lady Vanessa was breathless with excitement. "I have read of cosmetics with special powers. I believe these cosmetologists may be trafficking in powerful aphrodisiacal potions. We must take care to win their confidence and obtain their most potent concoctions."

But on their way to Dragon's Heart Nail Spa, the two women spied a new storefront with a strange name and wares that immediately left Lady Vanessa perplexed.

"Pilates? What is this?" she said after reading the name Premiere Pilates on the window.

"I think it's like yoga or something," said Magdalena.

Lady Vanessa pressed her face to the window and peered in.

"Pilate is the name of the man who betrayed Jesus, my dear Magdalena. If I'm not mistaken, this must be some kind of cult dedicated to the worship of Satan."

"Here? In Manhattan? Are you crazy?"

"Never more lucid in all my days. Oh, my goodness! Look!"

The two women peered into the window and were shocked to see handsome Nelson Dodge with his arms gripping a steel exercise contraption while his feet, sheathed in straps, turned tiny circles in the air. A tall, muscular woman wearing tights and a skimpy sleeveless t-shirt that exposed her bare, well-muscled arms and midriff stood over him as he toiled.

"It's Nelson!" cried Lady Vanessa. "He must have unwittingly fallen into their trap. Look, he's tied up and being tortured! I can barely stand to watch him grimacing in pain!"

"I think he's really doing exercise. Like a gym, you know?"

"Oh, please, Magdalena! It's torture, clear as day. It could be one step before human sacrifice, for all we know. Satanists love to offer fresh flesh to the devil. It's all in Maxine Payne's *Devil's Lust*, where young, pure Agatha is nearly seduced into joining a bloodthirsty Luciferious cult."

"But Lady Vee, if it was devil worship and torture, why would they do this in the window where everyone can see?"

"Being kind, good-hearted, relatively chaste maidens, we have no idea how these heretics think. Quickly! There's no time to waste!"

Lady Vanessa pushed open the door to Premiere Pilates and pointed at the tall instructor. "How dare you? Release that poor man at once!"

"Excuse me," said the instructor, stepping away from the bizarre-looking intruder in a hoop skirt before her. "We're in the middle of a private session here."

"Don't worry, Nelson," Lady Vanessa said. "We'll get you out of there!"

Nelson, who was not wearing his contact lenses, squinted. "Vanessa, is that you?"

"Yes, my sweet. And not a moment too soon." She grabbed Nelson's foot and pulled off the foot strap. "There, you are free from this sick satanic ritual."

"What are you doing?" thundered the instructor.

"Vanessa...." said Nelson.

"Do you know this wacko?"

"She lives in my building."

"I am Lady Vanessa of Manhattanshire!" declared Her Ladyship in as regal a voice as possible. "And this is my lady-in-waiting, Magdalena."

"Vanessa! This is an *exercise* session. I'm paying a hundred and twenty dollars to get my core in shape," said Nelson, smacking his stomach.

"While I adore your core, I believe these Jesus-haters will weaken your soul."

"Jesus-haters? Is she on drugs?" asked the instructor.

"Don't play innocent. It's obvious you are evangelizing the exercises of Pontius Pilate, the man who condemned Jesus to the cross!"

"Ooh, that's some bad stuff," said Magdalena.

"Not 'Pilate'!" yelled the instructor. "'Pi-lah-*teez*'! It's a German exercise! It has nothing to do with the guy in the Bible!"

Nelson Dodge was standing up now. "Look, Vanessa, this is not what you think it is. I'm just working out. This is like a gym with some very specialized equipment."

"Has this she-devil already cast her spell, Nelson? I can see how such a dominatrix might enchant you with such kinky devices, and I can't blame you. I myself have been known to engage in playful passion—my safe word is algebra, by the way."

"*Safe word?*" said the instructor. "Nelson, is she really your friend? Because I'm about to call the cops."

Nelson grabbed Lady Vanessa's elbow and started to steer her toward the door. "Vanessa, dear, I'm afraid you've misinterpreted the situation. This is a legitimate exercise studio. And I assure you there is zero chance of hanky-panky between me and Alexandra."

"Oh, come now, Nelson. I'm an adult. I can see the erotic appeal."

"Earth to Vanessa," Nelson said, smiling. "Nelson Dodge here! Single man with a small black poodle! Trust me, erotic appeal lies elsewhere."

And with those words, he steered a bewildered Lady Vanessa out the door. Then he turned to Magdalena, who had stopped to pick up a Premiere Pilates promotional flyer, and guided the lady-in-waiting out as well, whispering, "Please look after her."

The door to Premiere Pilates closed behind them, but Lady Vanessa was determined to have the last word.

"Be strong, Nelson!" she called through the glass, pounding on it with her fists. "We can repel Beelzebub's wicked delights! Rest assured; I shall provide you with a silver chalice to defeat that wanton temptress of the underworld!"

TRANSLATOR'S NOTE #2

At this point in the novel I may owe some readers a clarification of sorts or, at the very least, some words of reassurance.

I am quite certain that some readers will by now have detected something vaguely familiar about the engaging tale that has unfolded so far. And some of you may be wondering about the high words of praise with which I introduced the book you hold in your hand. "How," you may ask, "can an esteemed literary figure of such renown as Oona Noor wax ecstatic about a book that owes its plot to one of the oldest novels known to mankind?"

I feel it is best to address the "overtones" and "shadows" that fill The Seductive Lady Vanessa of Manhattanshire. *Indeed, very specific plot points do, unquestionably, mimic a well-known previous work, a classic tome that celebrates a delusional main character obsessed with certain books who hires a rotund sidekick who is equal measures faithful, idiotic, incredulous, and above all hopeful that the protagonist will lead the way to happiness. And that wonderful story also makes mention of an adoring relative who banishes the books beloved by the protagonist in an attempt to stop his madness.*

And the previous chapter, in which our heroine mistakes exercise equipment as torture devices of the devil, may remind readers of a certain well-known episode about a man who attacks a windmill he believes to be a monster.

If what you have read does not stir up any of these kinds of associations, dear reader, then great! You are advised to skip the rest of this note and keep reading the work of the mysterious Ms. Aisha Benengeli.

If, however, you are nodding to yourself at this very moment and thinking, "Yes, this book is clearly a rip-off of Miguel de Cervantes's unmatchable, groundbreaking, hilarious, and timeless comic novel, The Adventures of Don Quixote, *then I implore you to grant me a few paragraphs of your time that I may make myself understood.*

I, too, am very aware that Benengeli is spinning a tale that owes a good deal to Cervantes. But it is my firm belief that this is no simple slight or lazily counterfeited fiction. Nor is it the work of a plagiarist author trying to pass off some great work as her own.

While the comedy and mirth evidenced in the first two chapters recall the uproarious foibles of the man of La Mancha and his sidekick Sancho Panza, they are still of great merit, displaying a surefire wit that traffics in satire, parody, double acts, and absurdity—and is yet grounded in a contemporary world that remains winningly plausible.

Indeed, literature is built on works of the past. Shakespeare, it is said, constructed numerous plays out of the shards of lesser material. And I know for a fact that Midnight at the Oasis, *the book that I translated to such heated and unanimous acclaim in 1997 when it was hailed as the "pinnacle of erotic Arabic literature" in* People *magazine, recast some older works that had circulated in the Nile Valley hundreds of years earlier. Did I believe for one second that the existence of these older tales diminished the lusty language and sultry scenarios of* Midnight at the Oasis*? No, I did not!*

And let me assure you—without revealing any spoilers—that Benengeli is a cogent, magnificent string-puller and a versatile and original voice. I beg readers to be patient, for this book moves in unexpected ways, and suffice it to say, Lady Vanessa's is not the only journey that comes into play.

To reveal more than this would be to sabotage the joy, the surprise, and the heartbreak that comes with the best in true romantic fiction.

CHAPTER 3

In which seductive powers of a most exotic kind are sought, and Lady Vanessa explains the double-wedding whammy

Shocked but not completely surprised by the discovery of an underworld portal masquerading as an exercise studio, where Nelson's very soul might be at risk—and more importantly to Lady Vanessa, her access to his noble and tender heart might be jeopardized—Lady Vanessa was visibly shaken.

"Lady Vee, don't worry," Magdalena said. "I really don't think that's a portal to hell."

"No one ever thinks portals to hell are portals to hell. That is why they are so hellish," Lady Vanessa said. "I am very worried."

"Well, Nelson really didn't seem to be in danger."

"You really think so?"

"Of course. He ain't leaving that dog of his behind, not even to party with Satan."

"That's an interesting point. He does love Trixie."

"You could take that to the bank, yo!"

Lady Vanessa nodded although she had no idea what Magdalena was going on about with her reference to a bank or someone named Yo. But she felt herself growing calmer about Nelson. Perhaps he was strong enough to ward off that evil exercise temptress. She and Magdalena hooked arms and proceeded to the Dragon's Heart Nail Salon.

On their way, Magdalena shared the news of her friend, Iris, who had recently become engaged after a visit to the Dragon's Heart, and she attributed her new status as a bride-to-be to the spellbinding allure of the salon's rare and unique lacquers.

"Before Iris came here," Magdalena testified about her betrothed pal, "Silvio was just playing her. He even tried to get with me. And I outweigh that skinny dawg by fifty pounds!"

"Don't underestimate your charms, dear Magdalena," Lady Vanessa admonished her young assistant. "The larger the woman, the greater the love, as has been written many times."

"Well, she came here, and she got Slinky Purple Leopard Dot, which is made from fur and urine harvested from a caged leopard at a Korean zoo. And that same night, Silvio was mad crazy about her. Buying her bling and flowers."

The two women arrived at the Dragon's Heart Nail Spa, and Lady Vanessa addressed one of the diminutive Asian women at the front desk. "Good day, fair artisan. We have come for your most amorous potions."

The proprietor squinted at the bizarrely dressed customer and her young friend.

"You want mani-pedi?"

"Yes, we do. But we have heard you have pigments with powerfully alluring qualities that will turn us into magnets for all male-dom."

The salon owner squinted again.

Magdalena saw her confusion. "She means, you got polishes with big-ass sexy ingredients."

"Oh, sexy, sexy polish! Yes! Here is special menu," said the owner, proffering a laminated sheet of paper. She looked to her left, then to her right, and leaned toward her customers in conspiratorial fashion. "But this is very secret. You no tell anybody, okay?"

"Did you understand a word, Magdalena?"

Magdalena took the plastic-covered menu and nodded. "Yes, we're getting the goods but don't tell no one."

"*Special imports,*" whispered the owner, waving Lady Vanessa and Magdalena closer. "*You will be irresistible. But top secret, okay?*"

Lady Vanessa's face lit up. "Agreed, madam. I will never breathe a word about your aphrodisiacs, lest other women find them to try to steal away my true love. Of course, your potions will ultimately be of no use to them for two logical reasons. First, if he is my true love, then no hussy will ever keep us apart, for he will know in his heart that I am the only woman for him despite the loose and alluringly slutty temptresses who will cross his path.

"Second, I am a rapacious, kinky, giving lover with a heart that beats steadily for a good, noble, decent man, and I will never be bested by tawdry tarts of the lowest, rankest order, even if they have used the unique offerings of your enchanting emporium."

The owner nodded blankly. She was used to strange, diva customers, and she wondered if the woman before her, dressed in someone's discarded Halloween costume, had perhaps escaped from an insane asylum or was on crack cocaine or some other mind-altering drug. But a customer was a customer. She said, "You pay first, okay?"

"Of course! I am Lady Vanessa of Manhattanshire!"

Lady Vanessa and Magdalena sat side by side to study the listing of supposedly smuggled nail paints. The exotic names included Slinky Purple Leopard Dot for eighty-five dollars, Tiger Urine Moon Lust for ninety dollars, and Zebra Skin Nectar, Ground Eland Horn with Monkey Gland, and Donkey Blood Love Potion all at a bargain price of seventy-five dollars.

"I want Slinky Purple, like my friend got," said Maggie.

"Are you sure? Monkey Gland sounds so exotic."

"Lady Vanessa, you know your own powers. But didn't you tell me you were very drawn to the moon?"

"You are so right! Tiger Urine Moon Lust seems tailor-made for me. And it's the most expensive."

"Try it! What could go wrong?"

"What do you think happens if you use two different lacquers?"

"You mean like putting a Monkey Musk dot on a Tiger Urine Moon Lust base?"

"Exactly."

"I don't know. It might make it stronger. But it might confuse things. We don't mix no wine coolers into our champagne, know what I'm sayin'?"

"I think that's right. You are a very bright girl sometimes, Magdalena. Like using two different perfumes at once, they can clash and leave you smelling like a harlot."

"Or a whore!"

"Oh, my dear Magdalena! A harlot *is* a more refined way of saying prostitute."

"Sorry. I didn't know."

"We learn from each other. For instance, I would never have known about these spellbinding lacquers if it weren't for you."

Magdalena nodded. "Word."

Lady Vanessa looked at her aide *d'amour* and waited for further elaboration. After a moment, she said, "What word?"

"That just means I like what you said, Lady Vee."

"Of course," laughed Lady Vanessa, masking her confusion. "Or rather, 'word.' Madame! Madame!" Lady Vanessa waved over the owner and informed her of their choices.

The proprietor barked orders at two elderly nail technicians, who guided Lady Vanessa and Magdalena to their respective chairs for footbaths. While they were being pampered, Magdalena reached into her bag for the flyer she'd picked up while beating a retreat from Premiere Pilates and started reading it.

"I don't see nothing about the underworld, Lady Vee," said Magdalena.

"Well, it's certainly not something you would advertise. I'm sure those underworld scoundrels use their forked tongues to spread hell on earth."

"But damn, it's true what he said. It cost a hundred and twenty *an hour!*"

"What?" Lady Vanessa was shocked. Perhaps Nelson, in addition to being dreamy and too old to want children, was also rich. She'd always hoped so, and the idea that he would fork out such a sizable amount certainly suggested he was a man of means.

"That's some serious *pirogues con salsa* right there! Some definite bank, yo!"

"Don't worry, dear. When we find our soulmates of seduction, concerns about money will be a thing of the past. Did I tell you? The other day I saw Nelson's good friend, Toby, who is much younger than Nelson and has a matching poodle and a red sports car. I believe he is what is known as 'very single.'"

"To show me is to know me," Magdalena said, winking at her boss.

At this, Lady Vanessa's enthusiastic smile, the expression of someone who is feeling entirely at ease and pleased, fell flat.

It was during moments like these, when Magdalena would make some incomprehensible statement, that Lady Vanessa wondered if the chunky Polish-Dominican gal was as insane as she was busty. This question bred more questions because if Magdalena was, in fact, a well-meaning moron, this simply would not do. She needed a reliable ally to steer her, to reel her back in when her powerful womanly passions would spin out of control, detonated by the irresistible, magnetic charm of some loin-melting Don Juan, some cunning Casanova. She needed a wing lady-in-waiting, as it were, who would spot the moment a love rival entered the scene and help wage the inevitable war for her man's heart.

Gradually, however, Lady Vanessa digested Magdalena's bizarre statement and realized this was doubtless some mangled translation of an ancient, thousand-year-old Polish adage or Spanish proverb that probably meant "please introduce me" without actually saying that.

A smile returned to Lady Vanessa's overly painted face, and she said, "Yes! I will definitely arrange an introduction, and then—"

"Yo, maybe we'll have a double wedding!"

"Oh, no, no, no, no, *no!*" declared Lady Vanessa. "Double weddings are for sisters only! Or on rare occasions, as in *I Do, I Do!* or *Magnum & Son* or *Four of Hearts*, a mother and daughter might share the altar. Otherwise, double weddings are strictly forbidden."

"Why?"

"Excuse me, lady," said the woman who had been painting Lady Vanessa's toenails. "We do mani now, okay?"

"Certainly," said Lady Vanessa.

When Magdalena joined her at the manicure tables and the two sat side by side, their fingertips soaking in shallow bowls of warm water, Lady Vanessa continued the conversation.

"Magdalena, you lovely butterball! I appreciate your remark about a double wedding, but I want to make sure you fully understand. Your wedding day should be your own. You don't want a dazzling, older-but-very-sexy woman like me stealing your thunder. All eyes should be on you and your gorgeous betrothed!"

"Is that in all them books?"

"It's practically an unwritten law."

"I just thought it would be fun."

"Fun? Yes. I suppose it might be that. But when you are about to join your heart in perfect, loving unity with the heart of a male specimen who will fulfill your every need and desire materially, physically, and emotionally, while all your friends are looking at you, seething with contradictory feelings of admiration and jealousy, you want to be the center of attention."

"Also, yo, I bet you get more better gifts. Like, if we was both getting married, we'd get half as good presents because people ain't busting the bank on two girls in one day."

"Yes, that is very clear in Porticia Portmanteau's *The Farrell Boys of Farrell Farm* because they are all just as broke at the end of their quadruple wedding as they were before exchanging vows. But there is some thought that Porticia needed to ensure they were broke so that she could write four more books to explain how each of the four couples finally rise to become the cream of society. But yes, double weddings, unless occurring at the upper echelons of society, are said to dilute dowries."

Magdalena squinted as she processed her lady's latest bizarre reference to a book she had never heard of by an author she had definitely never heard of. Then she nodded and decided to change the subject.

"How are you feeling with your nails, Lady Vee?"

The middle-aged woman, her bonnet askew, held the back of her hands up before her eyes and beamed. "My blood is running hot!"

"Mine's, too."

CHAPTER 4

In which Lady Vanessa lures a vagabond, and the two beauties dine on love

The two women decided to head home with their freshly lacquered nails and attempt to put their new bewitching charms to use.

"I feel so alluring. As if I'm a walking, talking, love amulet!" Lady Vanessa declared.

"I know, right? I feel like every man I see is mentally undressing me."

"Oh my!"

"And the ones that like real women, not skinny-ass girls, is staring mad hard at me, you know?"

"If you wish to cling to that illusion, I will not attempt to dissuade you, Magdalena. But the good woman at the spa told me my nail polish and design is the most powerful."

"That's what *my* spa lady told me! She said my nails turned her into a *lesbian*!"

"Oh please! She was just buttering you up for a bigger tip, Magdalena. It's a common practice."

"How about you? It's the same for you. That bitch who did your nails just wanted a bigger tip!"

"My lacquer was the most expensive on the menu. That means my nails have more charm power. It's basic supply-and-demand logic. When Diamond Douglaston in *Fortress of Fortune* wanted to woo General Patrick Ryan, she didn't spray herself with Febreze, she went straight for Chanel No. 5. And that's a lesson all ladies must learn. Never skimp."

Instantly, Magdalena felt a rage brewing over Lady Vanessa's insulting logic. Not everyone could afford to skip skimping. For a brief moment she considered storming off and telling her weirdo employer where she could put her Chanel No. 5, but then she thought about Nelson's "very single" friend Toby and his little dog, and the fact that Nelson seemed to have lots of money and perhaps his friend had lots of money too.

Sometimes she doubted Lady Vanessa's wisdom, but she had never known anyone who had read or owned so many books—despite the considerable purge of titles by her daughter and the neighbors, Lady Vanessa's apartment was still overrun by the romances—or who talked with such self-assurance about the world. Maggie had asked her cousin, an elementary school teacher, if she knew other people with apartments full of books.

"The rents are higher than a crackhead in this town," her cousin had said. "Who has room for books?"

So even though Lady Vanessa could be stuck up and insulting, especially about Magdalena's weight, the lady-in-waiting felt tied to her mistress and her ways—especially her promise to help her find true love with a guy with mad bank.

And hadn't the old bag just paid for Magdalena's own super-sexy nails?

"Okay, yours is nice, boss. Nicer than mines. I'm just saying I'm feeling the power."

"That's quite alright, Magdalena. Our auras are undeniable."

At that moment, an obviously inebriated man lurched in their direction, flashing a leering, broken-toothed smile as he stuck out his hand.

"Can you help a man in need, ma'am?"

"Oh! See?" Lady Vanessa turned to Magdalena. "Our allure is obviously intoxicating. He is so consumed with desire he can barely walk!"

"Anything will do," said the man.

"He's desperate for us," whispered Lady Vanessa.

Magdalena whispered back. "He's a bum. He's drunk. He just wants money."

"Nonsense!" declared Lady Vanessa, turning to the down-and-out-panhandler. "Would you like to accompany us?"

The drunk eyed her warily. He was used to being avoided, not engaged. He suspected these women were Christians who would try to take him to a church—the last place he wanted to go.

"You wouldn't happen to be Seventh Day Adventists?" he slurred.

"What? No! I am Lady Vanessa of Manhattanshire, and this is Magdalena, my lady-in-waiting."

"I've been waiting too. For you. I'm a prince! Fallen on hard times."

"If he's a prince, Lady Vee, then I'm Angelina Jolie," said Magdalena. "You can smell the booze coming out of his skin!"

But Lady Vanessa was too busy piecing together the evidence, as only her encyclopedic and delusional mind could see it.

"Magdalena, do you not remember *The Lost Prince* by Elsbeth Mercy or *The Pauper's Revenge* by Constance Appleby? Or *The Fallen King* by Daphne Du Monde?"

"No, Lady Vee. You know I only read your alpha male and Marines books."

"These were all stories of gallant teenage monarchs who pledged their love to fair maidens but were ripped from their paramours and removed from their birthright by wicked uncles, power-mad counselors, and dastardly younger brothers, stripped of their destiny to lead by rank cowards and then banished, forced to live in exile, enduring years of humiliating poverty and hunger, and yet through it all they bravely plotted their return, steadfastly working in the shadows to obtain sweet vengeance and a blissful reunion with their true first loves."

"But this guy is obviously drunk, Lady Vee. And don't princes have all their teeth?"

"Drunk? Me?" laughed the drunk. "I ain't *begun* to get started!"

"Tell me, fine sir," asked Vanessa. "Where did you reign?"

"Rain? Last night it was pouring. I spent it under the Manhattan Bridge, me and Rico and some dudes with zombie weed. That shit'll get you through a hurricane. It *is* a hurricane."

"You miss my meaning. Where are you from?"

"Me? Kensington."

"Kensington! Do you hear this, Magdalena? Dear God, do my ears deceive me?"

"He means Kensington in Brooklyn, Lady Vee. Not, like, Scotland or wherever you think that is."

"Nonsense!"

"Does he sound like Hugh Grant or that old geezer... Sean Connery?"

The soused panhandler weaved closer to Lady Vanessa and a breeze carried his alcohol-soaked stench toward her. Shocked by the noxious alcohol and body odor bouquet, she took a step back. Suddenly, her blotto suitor went sprawling to the curb and began to vomit.

"See?" said Magdalena in disgust. "I told you he's drunk."

"Not necessarily! In *Prince Vagabond*, by Mercedes Porsche, the banished prince also has black magic hex of the stomach, which forces him to live on only bread, water, and chili peppers."

"This guy don't smell like that. He smells like a dive bar bathroom with a backed-up toilet, yo!"

Just then, a police officer walked by and stood over the regurgitating reprobate, nudging the man with his nightstick. "Is this guy bothering you, ladies?"

Lady Vanessa batted her lashes and held her fingers to her mouth as she stifled a giggle, the better to show off her enchanting fingernail polish. "Oh no, not at all, officer. We were just about to cross the street."

And with that, Lady Vanessa locked arms with Magdalena and continued their journey home.

Lady Vanessa and her lady-in-waiting Magdalena Stanislaw Cruz were still giddy over the supposed bewitching powers of their overpriced Korean nail polish. But the allegedly aphrodisiac-laced lacquers did nothing to quell mountainous Magdalena's lust for food, and she mentioned she was hungry.

The two women were just a block from Lady Vanessa's apartment, and Lady Vanessa was about to launch into a diatribe on the values of dieting and self-restraint, especially for young, strapping Polish-Dominican-American girls like Magdalena, when she spied a familiar well-coiffed head and immaculate mustache in the window of a local diner.

It was Nelson Dodge!

And instead of that dreadful Pilates temptress who had been so obviously intent on leading Nelson to the underworld, he was sitting with another man. A younger man in a neon-blue, sleeveless buttoned-down and collared shirt, the likes of which Lady Vanessa could not recall ever seeing but of which she wholeheartedly approved, especially the way it showed off the man's well-muscled arms.

"Certainly, Magdalena!" she declared, tabling her lecture for another day. "Let us celebrate our cunning decorative concoctions with a light repast at Leonard's Diner."

The two women entered the restaurant and Nelson, who had just finished explaining to his young friend Fabian how his Pilates session had been interrupted by a crazed neighbor who for some inexplicable reason thought he was involved in black magic cult, slapped his head. "Oh my god, it's her!"

Fabian immediately turned to look, and Nelson realized his error. "Don't look, don't look, don't look," he said under his breath while also staring intently at his cell phone and praying Vanessa hadn't actually seen him.

But of course that was not to be.

"Nelson!" erupted Lady Vanessa, rushing over to the table. "Thank goodness you made it out of that she-devil's torture chamber! We were so worried."

Nelson looked up from his phone, gave an exasperated eye roll to Fabian, and said, "Vanessa, I'm just going to say two things. First, I pay *a lot* of money for that class, and I do *not* want to be interrupted there ever again. Second, there is nothing evil or torturous about that class. It's exercise! Now, I'm going to try and forget that ever happened, so we can go back to being pals."

"I told her it was like yoga with machines," said Magdalena.

"Exactly! Although it's far better than yoga, if you want to know the truth."

Lady Vanessa resisted the impulse to smack her faithful servant for publicly speaking against her mistress, and instead forced an ebullient smile to her lips. "Excuse our rudeness," she said, turning to Nelson's friend. "My name is Lady Vanessa and this fair maiden, full of figure, vim, and charm, is Magdalena, my lady-in-waiting."

"Nice to meet you," said Fabian, sliding farther into the booth. "My name is Fabian Husk. Would you care to join us?"

Lady Vanessa quickly filled the space created by Fabian and gave Nelson a commanding wave to scoot over for Magdalena.

Once they were seated, Lady Vanessa looked over at Magdalena and realized a new crisis now loomed before her.

The massive young woman, who only minutes earlier had pronounced herself starving, was about to order her normal, excessively large meal in front of the sculpted, zero-body-fat magnificence of Fabian Husk. She foresaw disaster: Any possibility of romance with the fetching Fabian would be squashed under Magdalena's inevitable, horrifying, cholesterol-saturated order of liver and onions with sides of kielbasa and potato salad, which Magdalena unironically referred to as "her greens."

Lady Vanessa thought about dashing off a text to her charge, but this would need to be explained carefully so as not to anger Magdalena, who was sensitive about any mention of her girth. Instead, as soon as a waitress dropped off menus for the new arrivals, Lady Vanessa opted to launch a preemptive strike. She smiled warmly at her lady-in-waiting and said, "Now, Magdalena, let us order just a snack as we have a banquet awaiting us this evening."

"We do?"

"Yes. Remember? The Bloomberg Foundation? Don't tell me you've forgotten."

"How can I remember something I never knew?"

"Oh dear!" laughed Lady Vanessa, looking at Nelson and Fabian. "I was certain I mentioned it to you. When the ex-mayor invites you to an event, it does tend to stick in the mind."

"Oh!" said Magdalena. "Damn. Is that why we got our nails done?"

"Oh my! Look at those lacquers," gushed Fabian, grabbing Lady Vanessa's hands. "*That* is a stunning paint job!"

Lady Vanessa felt herself going flush. She wished it was Nelson who was studying her intoxicating nail polish, but the touch of Fabian's massive hand *was* exciting.

"I got mine's done too," said Magdalena, holding the back of her hands in front of Nelson for his appraisal.

Nelson put his fork down and pulled his seatmate's large paws toward him.

"Oh, my! You have some serious digits here."

"Thank you."

"And the colors are spectacular."

A waitress approached the table. "Are you ready to order?"

"Oh yes, I'm starving," said Magdalena.

"We'll each have the soup and salad," said Lady Vanessa, quickly handing the waitress the menu in the hope that she would leave before Magdalena corrected her. But, to her dismay, no such luck.

"Wait. I'll have the liver and onions."

"Magdalena! Don't forget the Bloomberg gala."

"I'll be able to eat there."

"Is that all?" asked the waitress.

"Oh my God," said Nelson, glancing at his phone. "Look at the time. We have to go. Can we get our check, please?"

The waitress made a few calculations and slammed the bill down on the table. "So, is it soup and salad or liver and onions?"

"Both," said Magdalena.

Nelson threw three tens on the table. "I'm so sorry, Vanessa. But Fabian and I have to get to the East Side for a meeting."

"I understand perfectly!" sang Lady Vanessa, who was delighted that the two handsome men would be spared the spectacle of Magdalena gorging herself on a plate brimming with food, not to mention a bowl of soup that inevitably would be subsumed by a cascade of crumbling crackers that her lady-in-waiting would crush while in their packets and then spill over the broth with a flourish.

"It was a pleasure to meet you both," said Fabian, as the women stood up to let the men extract themselves from the booth. "And really, your nails are just too, also, and more!"

As soon as the men departed, Magdalena grabbed a napkin and began patting her forehead with it. "Oh my god, Lady Vanessa! Did you hear that? He loved my nails."

"Your nails? I believe he was referring to the lacquers gracing both our hands."

"He said they were *tooalsoandmore*!" Magdalena squealed. "He was so hot! Oh, Lady Vee, you were so right!"

"Now Magdalena, please try to control yourself. We really don't know anything about Fabian Husk. Where he's from, who his family is, what he does for a living. And most importantly"—Her Ladyship leaned over the table to get closer to Magdalena so she could whisper—"we don't know *anything about his past.*"

"But surely—"

"Surely nothing! Is there not an entire library filled with cads and cowards who led maidens on, spinning, pledging, vowing, waxing, wooing, hinting, promising, and declaring, only to leave them broken and wretched?"

"I suppose so...."

"*You suppose*! As your Lady, I command you to suspend your passion for Fabian until we know more."

"But—"

"Magdalena Cruz, I insist!"

"Okay, Lady Vee. I'll keep everything in check. At least till the banquet."

The waitress placed their orders in front of them with brusque efficiency. The loud plunks made Lady Vanessa close her eyes in distaste. Then she opened them. "The banquet? Oh dear. I think I got my dates wrong with that." She sighed. "Eat all you want, my dear."

TRANSLATOR'S NOTE #3

Here the original manuscript by the mysterious Aisha Benengeli ends. The title page of the document I was sent, however, clearly states the work is a "riwaya," the Arabic word for novel.

Reaching this sudden vanishing point, my head was filled with urgent questions. Was this story, as the ancient saying goes, merely a grain of sand at the start of the desert? Were there more pages to this mesmerizing work? Or was this as far as the author got, for, as every writing group member knows, an infinite number of unfinished novels lurk in the bowels of countless computer hard drives and desk drawers.

I refused to believe that such a masterful writer would quit after such an engaging start. Therefore, I conducted countless searches for Aisha Benengeli via the internet. I even appealed to an attaché at the Egyptian Consulate in New York to help me ferret out the Benengeli population in Cairo and Alexandria, where I was sure such an accomplished author would most likely be based.

Alas, my search entries and formal queries yielded no relevant information. I found a few Benengelis on Facebook, but my exchanges with them turned up nothing. No one, it seemed, had ever heard of an Aisha Benengeli.

Disappointed but still fascinated, I was determined to discover if missing pages existed and, if they did, to find them at all costs. I got on a plane and flew to the hot, overstuffed city of Cairo to continue my search. I alerted local book dealers and collectors of Arabic and English literary flotsam and jetsam to be on the lookout for any further adventures of Lady Vanessa or any writings by the mysterious Aisha Benengeli.

My second order of business was to contact Sadeki Salah, the kind soul who found the manuscript and mailed it to me. Unfortunately, I was told Mr. Salah was away on a business trip to London and would not return for another two weeks.

I passed some time in my hotel, waiting for my network of rare manuscript collectors to respond to me, knowing full well I would receive a number of forged and bogus documents. Having provided dealers with the name Aisha Benengeli, it was now assured that certain shady characters would create manuscripts and papers adorned with Aisha's alluring name on otherwise shoddy work. This was the way of the souk and its population of the hustlers desperate to make a living in that hellaciously hot, dusty, and claustrophobic city. These semiliterate hucksters would visit and joke that there is a souk-ah born every minute and then laugh their heads off over that groan-inspiring joke, which, of course, also served as a veiled admission of their true intent: to make a sucker out of me. Fortunately, while I am an American, I speak the language and know the culture, thanks to my parents who were born in Karnak. Many of these would-be scammers did not know who they were dealing with, nor, being so poorly educated, had they ever heard of, much less read, Ali Bin Dawad's The Trader with Two Mouths, *with its famous opening line: "Never con a conman." Which is not to say I am a conman, or rather, conwoman, but that I am aware of the hard-working fraudsters and fiends who circulate in a Cairo souk in search of a dishonest buck.*

Despite my simultaneous and contradictory contempt and admiration for my bibliophilic ferreters and their contempt and undoubted admiration for me, my desire to learn more about this tantalizing work of humor and eros was so powerful that, after the manuscript of my dreams failed to turn up, I decided to offer a reward to provide further motivation: $5,000 to anyone who found the rest of the manuscript.

This resulted in another slew of submissions brought to my hotel by money-hungry emissaries. Unfortunately and predictably, the so-called discoveries were nothing more than dreck of the lowest order.

After two weeks and three dozen unspeakably bad manuscripts presented to me, Mr. Sadeki Salah returned from his trip. Together, we decided to visit the Khan el-Khalili bazaar, where my initial correspondent found the manuscript. The original vendor, Ali Mohammed, was dead, we were told. Apparently, on a visit to his ancestral village up the Nile, he had a heart attack while watching a series of camel races and placing a large bet on the winning beast. Tragically, Mr. Mohammed did not survive to collect his winnings. At any rate, I asked Sadeki to find out who took over Ali Mohammed's estate. The owner of a neighboring souk stall volunteered that Ali Mohammed's well-to-do cousin had cleared out his space. The concerned gentleman said he would love to introduce me but that he would lose a great deal of money if he closed his shop to lead me to the cousin's posh store, where he believed Ali Mohammad's wares had been relocated. I offered the man fifty dollars to do just that and thanked Mr. Salah for his help. My new guide then hailed a cab and, after an interminable forty-five minute ride, deposited me outside a men's clothing shop owned by Anwar Mohammed in Nasr City, a high rise-filled section of Cairo.

"Would you like to see our newest suit from Versace?" a well-dressed shop assistant shod in gleaming Italian loafers asked as I entered the shop.

I explained that although I admired Versace, I was more interested in meeting the store owner.

In seconds, Mr. Anwar Mohammed appeared from the back of his delightfully air-conditioned shop. We exchanged salaams, and Mr. Mohammed offered me coffee and a seat.

I took up his kind offer and then told him about the Yves Saint Laurent bag Sadeki Salah had purchased from his late cousin and the intriguing manuscript that was found within. Anwar Mohammed thought for a moment and then made a phone call. I looked elsewhere while he yelled into the phone, ordering whoever was on the other end to get down to the store immediately.

"My daughter," he explained after hanging up.

Five minutes later, a young woman and her younger brother appeared at the store. They looked nervous, no doubt because of their father's brusque tone.

"The papers you took from Uncle Ali's home, the ones Auntie Miriam was saving—do you still have them?"

The girl shook her head.

"Nadia has them."

"Yassir!"

The shop assistant with the shiny shoes leapt to attention.

"Yes, boss?"

"Tell your wife to bring the manuscript she borrowed from Amina. Now!" Then he turned to me and said, "I didn't think his wife knew how to read."

Twenty minutes later, I had the manuscript before me, my extensive and desperate efforts thankfully rewarded. Mr. Mohammed praised Allah for this amazing discovery. And he praised Allah again when I presented him with a check for $5,000—the reward I had promised—to distribute as he saw fit, knowing he would likely distribute it to his own bank account. I was absolutely elated. My trip to Cairo, the ancient city that survives on the patience and poverty of its eighteen million sweating citizens, had miraculously ended in triumph. I flew back to New York and set to translating this most fascinating tale of love and lunacy.

Or is that last phrase redundant?

CHAPTER 5

In which Lady Vanessa sets out on a grand adventure that leads to the underworld

On a sunny day in September, Lady Vanessa woke up with charity in her heart and a benevolent idea in her head, both the result of the previous day's exchange with Magdalena, who had bemoaned the lack of suitable suitors in her life and the equal lack of unsuitable ones.

"I haven't had a date in months!" she complained. "And honestly, Lady Vee, neither have you. Never mind finding Mr. Right. I'll take Mr. Maybe, Mr. Maybe Not, or even Mr. One-and-Done."

"I don't know the gentlemen you are referring to," Lady Vanessa responded, "but you must realize I am still recovering from that infernal incident with Mr. Grey. And I have pledged myself to Nelson, as you well know."

"I know you have, and you know you have, but I'm not sure Nelson knows you have, my lady. He seems to only have eyes for his dog and Fabian."

Shocked by Magdalena's level of insolence, Lady Vanessa had risen from the kitchen table and declared, "I have no more use of your services today, Magdalena. Good evening." Then she marched into her room, slamming the door behind her for emphasis.

But this morning, Lady Vanessa felt motivated by her gigantic lady-in-waiting's single status.

It was clear the poor, uncultured Polish-Dominican giant-ess was simply a victim of her cloistered, outer-borough igno-rance, her pedestrian face, and her utter cluelessness when it came to the infinitely complex world of romance. And as Lady Vanessa was an expert on the five "Cs of Romance"—Courtship, Comportment, Coquetry, Concupiscence, and Cunning—she realized it was her duty to instruct her charge in the basics when it came to the formation of alliances and dangerous liaisons.

"Even though you have no position in society without your connection to me," Lady Vanessa said, speaking to the top of Magdalena's head while her lady-in-waiting was on her knees scrubbing the kitchen floor, "many maidens have overcome far greater obstacles and blackened pasts than you. So, come! Today we will go in search of worthy men."

"What's your definition of worthy, my lady? I got a great aunt. She's eighty-seven and she says all she wants is a guy who's breathing and can get to the bathroom by himself. End of story, yo!"

"Worthy? Surely you have a list of superior qualities that would set your heart aflutter."

"You mean like bling, right? Yes. Tattoos, muscles, and some nice jewelry are a turn on. Like a gold grille in the mouth. Yeah, that gets *my* motor running."

Lady Vanessa smiled weakly at what she viewed as her young associate's déclassé tastes, suppressing her horror only because she was determined to show Magdalena proper comportment.

"Others might find meritorious qualities in such things as place in society, kindness, grace under extreme duress, and handsomeness. I personally also find good manners a huge, as you might put it, turn on. These, for instance, are the qualities that ignited so many of the world's greatest romances."

"That sounds good. But where do you find those guys? The dudes I know, they so hard up for bank, they below lower class!"

"It's very simple. There is a place called the East Side of New York."

"What? Just across town?"

"Indeed. Although the West Side may have recently become the more desirable locale for many, the East Side is still where men of means abound. It is a veritable Manhattanshire of the Gods. Finish your cleaning and let us depart."

⚜

Lady Vanessa had a new ensemble for the occasion. In her mind, going after old money required a sophisticated, older look. Fortunately for her, a few days earlier, she had discovered a discarded birdcage in the basement of her building. She brought it upstairs and through careful hacking and bending, altered the cage wires to fashion a carriage for a new hoop skirt. In truth, although it was a considerable improvement on her original lampshade dress (which Emma had thrown out after her run-in with Christian Grey) and sturdier than the ratty hoop skirt she had found at the Thespians of Broadway sale, it still left much to be desired, for instead of swelling proudly, extending her derriere, it sagged. But when Lady Vanessa paraded before her mirror, she saw a shapely, daringly beautiful woman clad in a farthingale that fit her like a proverbial glove. The fact that said glove was more an oven mitten escaped her entirely.

After Magdalena finished scrubbing the floors and changed out of her cleaning clothes, Lady Vanessa appeared from her bedroom bedecked in her new togs.

"Wow!" gushed Magdalena, "that is some dress."

"A hoop skirt, Magdalena," said Lady Vanessa, twirling.

"Watch out!"

Her artificially amplified-but-sagging derriere knocked into a lamp, sending it flying.

"Oh dear, I shall have to get used to my new chassis."

"You got a mad hype Kardashian butt now. Damn, and you don't gotta pay no hundred thousand big ones on surgery!"

"Yes, I fashioned it myself."

"I know. You can't just get one of these at Old Navy, yo!"

The response endeared Lady Vanessa to her young lady-in-waiting, and she decided that instead of going directly to Fifth Avenue by taxi, they would make a leisurely promenade through Central Park.

It was a glorious day. And the twosome—a painted lady sprung from the pages of *Moll Flanders* and her towering, buxom accomplice—strolled arm in arm, winding around the ponds, athletic fields, and playgrounds of the park until they came to the famous model boat pond just south of the Metropolitan Museum of Art.

"Damn, I know this place!" said Magdalena.

"Yes, I can imagine you've been here before."

"No. Never. But I seen it in that movie about a mouse. *Stuart Little.*"

"Oh, yes, of course."

As they paused to admire the sophisticated remote-control models and simpler, wooden miniature ships crisscrossing the pond, they heard weeping behind them. On a bench, a handsome, well-dressed young man with a head of irresistible curls and sorrowful dark eyes sobbed uncontrollably into a large white handkerchief.

"Young man!" said Lady Vanessa, carefully hitching up the skirt hoops below her hips while sticking her butt out to sit on the bench beside the youth. "Whatever is the matter?"

The tearful young man continued his weeping, and Her Ladyship grew more concerned. She put a hand on his tightly blue-jeaned thigh.

"Should we call an ambulance? Or the police?"

He shook his head, and his outpouring of grief slowed. He looked at Lady Vanessa and then at the concerned giantess looming in front of him and wondered if he should bolt.

"No?" continued Lady Vanessa, speaking in a soothing tone. "Can you share why your heart breaks? I can only imagine one thing that could cause so much agony for someone so young."

"What?" asked Magdalena.

"Love! I suspect we are seeing a youthful and pure spirit torn apart at the heart. Is this true? Tell us!"

The be-snotted twenty-something on the bench nodded.

"A man with a broken heart is well served by sharing his heartbreak with other maidens," said Lady Vanessa. "Please. Recount your story. We are all ears, and rest assured our hearts and minds will ache with you."

"But I don't even know you," said the young man.

"That's okay. We don't even know you, neither," said Magdalena.

"Consider us blank slates. Fill us with your tale and we will offer our sympathy and counsel," said Lady Vanessa. "On my honor as Lady Vanessa of Manhattanshire, I pledge compassion, discretion, and decency."

The young man honked his nose into his hanky, then sighed as he folded it up and said, "Very well. But it's a long story."

"You have our undivided attention," said Lady Vanessa, looking to Magdalena for confirmation.

The latter nodded eagerly. "Lady Vanessa is a love guru, yo! If anyone can help you, it's her."

The young man looked far from convinced. But he sighed and in a shaky voice began his tale.

"Her name was Autumn. It was the perfect name. She had red hair and green eyes and a few orange freckles below her eyes. And she had full lips that were dark red. It may sound ridiculous, but she looked like the season she was named after."

"Oh dear," cried Lady Vanessa, who knew a foreshadowing when she heard one. "But another word for Autumn is *fall*!"

The young man ignored Lady Vanessa's analytical point and carried on as if in a trance.

"Her face was open. Calm and accepting, the way you feel after a hot summer finally ends, and the leaves and the temperature change. Everything about her was lovely and charming when we first met...at this exact spot.

"I was instantly spellbound. She was slender, with the kind of beauty and innocence that made me worry she might be preyed on by men with not-so-honorable intent, if you know what I mean."

Here, he looked up to receive confirmation from the women, who both nodded in utter earnestness to indicate that they knew *exactly* what kind of male he meant.

"And so," he continued, "I wanted to take her somewhere warm and safe and hidden from those others."

"It was love at first sight, right?" said Magdalena, turning to Lady Vanessa. "Like what you're always talking about."

"Quiet, please, Magdalena. Let him continue."

"The irony is that my feelings proved to be justified. If she seemed quiet and secretive it was because, I eventually discovered, she was leaving me."

"Another foreshadowing," whispered Lady Vanessa.

"I'd never felt anything like it." The young man swallowed, fighting back another deluge of tears. "We spent the whole evening together, walking in the park. It was magical. We..." The young man blushed.

Lady Vanessa whispered, "It's okay. We understand. We are specialists in love in all its expressions."

At this, the young man, completely unsure what, exactly, the bizarre-looking woman in front of him meant by such a statement—was she a deranged prostitute?—turned a brighter shade of red.

Lady Vanessa realized the youth before her was confused. "I have read more books on the life-bestowing subject of romance than an army of librarians," she declared by way of explanation.

The lovelorn lad nodded, although he wasn't sure how this fact was relevant, and resumed his story.

"That night, I didn't sleep. I just held her and watched the gorgeous miracle in my arms. But in the morning, she told me she was heartbroken. She would be leaving soon, and though she loved me with all her heart and felt we were perfect soul mates, she had to go to a place I could not follow."

"What, like jail?" asked Magdalena. "Damn, my ex-boyfriend Julio got five years, and he told me I could take the bus to see him. I said later for that!"

"I suppose, in a manner of speaking, it was jail, only worse," said the young man. "She began to tell me a story. But for the first time since I met her, she seemed hesitant and guarded. Now, I'm sure that was because she was making the story up as she went. She said she had joined the Peace Corps, just rented her apartment and had broken up a few months earlier with another guy to prepare herself for years of being lonely."

"You could have gone with her!" said Lady Vanessa.

"That's what I said. I said I'd go with her to Afghanistan, Pakistan, or whatever 'stan she was heading to. I didn't care. She was perfect."

At the memory of Autumn's beauty, he fought back more tears, took a deep breath, and steeled himself.

"Then she told me the horrible truth. Although now I'm not sure it was the truth at all."

"Yo, I bet she said she had, like, cancer or AIDS, right?"

"Magdalena, if you say one more word, I shall fire you immediately and you will never cast eyes on Nelson's friend Fabian again. Let this wretched young prisoner of love speak!"

The young man sighed once more.

Lady Vanessa saw the pain coursing through his face and was determined to help him. "Young squire," she said. "My name is Lady Vanessa. And I will pledge to use all my powers, notions, and vast knowledge of the quest for true love to help you. But first I require your name."

"Lance."

Instantly, Lady Vanessa felt herself blush to the roots of her hair. This was a name she dreamed about frequently. It was, to her mind, the most erotic name in the whole of the Book of Names, that epic compendium described in Hester Virginie's masterful twelve-novel "HeartQuest" series, the seventh volume of which, *The Royal Foundling*, famously lists six hundred men's names and the meanings behind them.

Lady Vanessa had read this dictionary of masculine monikers multiple times, pouring through the names in a fever dream of imaginary suitors parading, preening, prancing, and pitching as they recited their names, some as a basso profundo, others in slinky, dangerous rasps, while still others spiked their names with mesmerizing foreign accents—singsong Luigis; yodeling Matthaises; lisping Luises; icy, unreachable Ivans—names and deliveries she could hear even now if she chose to summon them.

But no name could ever match the clipped nobility of Lance. Not just a name but a verb and noun! A verb with a symbolic and unabashed, predatory, piercing carnality! And now, here before her, this frail, love-wounded young man bore the most heroic, most masculine name of all time! A true knight!

"You don't like my name?" said Lance.

"Oh, no! On the contrary, it is very dear to me," said Lady Vanessa, still blushing. She grabbed his arm. "It suits you well. Pray, proceed with your tale."

Lance nodded, swallowed, and pressed on.

"It took some time to get the story out of her, and even then, it made no sense. She told me she was from the underworld and had been sent here on a mission to irrevocably break a heart. Her cruel overlord, a hellish demon named Diblood, commanded her to come to earth to work off her brother's debt.

"She cried as she told me she'd succeeded in breaking her last boyfriend's heart in so many pieces that he committed suicide."

"Damn," said Magdalena. "What did she do to him?"

"She did what she was doing to me, she said. She spun her magic and he plummeted, trapped by her beauty and her open, sincere, caring manner."

"That never works for me."

"Magdalena!"

"She told me all this because she felt we had an instant connection and she didn't want to see me like her old boyfriend, tortured by cruelty that she could not control, despite her true feelings."

Lady Vanessa slapped her forehead, for she recognized elements of this tale as if she herself had lived through the very same story.

"A portal!" she yelled. "You need a portal to rescue her!"

The boy looked at her as though she were a madwoman.

"It's in *The Hounds of Love* by Constance Pierre!" Lady Vanessa said as if that explained everything.

"Is she nuts?" Lance asked Magdalena.

"Monique was sent here on the exact same mission by a hellhound named Lexter, a madman who sank his teeth into Saint O'Grady and was awarded a gift from Satan: an underworld lair of the lowest depths filled with love's saddest prisoners, humans who spend eternity as dogs, including the beautiful Samantha," explained Lady Vanessa.

"What are you babbling about?" said Lance. "What does any of that have to do with Autumn?"

"I'm trying to tell you! In *Hounds of Love*, Samantha has been exiled to Lexter's evil den of despair and is sent back to earth in her divine human form to woo and wound men. When her love victims were destroyed, she would return to her cruel underworld.

"But one man was strong enough to survive her charms and heartbreaking rejections—Connor Van Bright. Although his heart was shattered into a million pieces, he did not shuffle off this mortal coil. He remained a lovelorn wreck, determined to find Samantha. When a palm reader explained his fate, he decided to go in search of his true love and bring her back to the land of the living."

"You think what Autumn said was really true? She wasn't just trying to get rid of me?"

"The similarities are uncanny. This is doubtless the same trial, you poor thing."

"Or maybe, like, this Autumn read the same book, you know?" said Magdalena.

This was, in fact, a most sensible observation. It seemed quite likely to Magdalena that Autumn was concocting a fantastic Dear John breakup story. But Lady Vanessa, gripped by the spirit of a classic paranormal love adventure, did not give it a second's thought. "You must follow her!" Lady Vanessa declared. "And retrieve her from the depths of Hades!"

Lady Vanessa stood up and looked around the park, searching for something. "You met her here," she said. "This must be a special place for her. Unless I miss my guess, she was contemplating her return when you met her. And that suggests there's a portal nearby."

"You mean like one of those toilet things? Port-a-John?" asked Magdalena, who was just as confused as Lance.

"No! No! No! A *portal!* A doorway that transports you from one world and time to another. We must find it, Lance. And you must go and rescue her!"

Lady Vanessa lifted her eyes northward, and they settled on Central Park's famous bronze sculpture of Alice in Wonderland that stood nearby. Instantly, she knew this was just the kind of netherworld lair where evil would lurk and subterranean gargoyles would surface in secret to wreak havoc, tripping children, casting spells, and even kidnapping innocents.

"The statue!" she cried. "Follow me!"

Lady Vanessa dashed toward the bronze landmark, which, as usual, had a small crowd around it. Day after day, for generations, thrilled children and tourists have stepped up on the metallic mushroom and posed with Alice, the White Rabbit, and the Mad Hatter for photographs.

Magdalena looked at a bewildered Lance. "We better keep an eye on her."

"Is she serious?"

"Serious as syphilis, boyee! Let's go."

Lady Vanessa, seized by the unassailable nobility of her mission—to help handsome, heartbroken Lance find his true love, Autumn, and free her from the sickening hexes of Satan's ally Lexter—rushed toward the statue.

"Excuse me! Please, children! Excuse me! Out of the way! This is an *emergency!*" she roared, weaving through the crowd of hovering parents.

She stood before the giant mushroom upon which Alice sat. To her left, a boy with snot leaking from his nose was holding on to the White Rabbit's ears. To her right, a tall boy was beating out a rhythm on the Mad Hatter's top hat. And directly in front of her, two small French girls had just climbed onto the giant center mushroom and were preparing to approach Alice.

Lady Vanessa struggled to step onto the mushroom that served as Alice's perch. Her inflexible hoop skirt banged against the metal, but she was undaunted. Her mind raced, and her eyes darted. She searched to find the entryway to the underworld that she was positive existed and that was almost assuredly near literature's favorite traveler to an alternate universe. Unable to step high enough, Vanessa sat down on the mushroom and rolled herself onto the bronzed fungus cap and toward Alice, nearly steamrolling the two little French girls.

"*Maman! Maman!*" cried the terrified girls.

"*Qui est cette vache?*" asked the girls' horrified mother. "*Policier! Policier!*"

"Don't worry! Don't worry. I am on a noble quest!" said Lady Vanessa, who was finding it difficult to stand up. Indeed, she needed to reach out and grab the Cheshire Cat in Alice's arms to pull herself up to a standing position.

"*Maman! Maman!*" wailed the panicked French girls once more, fleeing into their mother's arms.

"Somebody call the cops!" yelled the boy beside the Mad Hatter. "This lady's crazy!"

"How dare you!" Lady Vanessa said, shooting a furious glare at the boy. "I am Lady Vanessa of Manhattanshire. And I am on a quest to aid dear Lance so that he may rescue his true love from the eternal fires and loveless agony of the underworld. There is no time to waste, and I must find the secret latch that will open the portal."

With that, she focused on the statue figures, grabbing at Alice's metalized hair, her nose, her shoulders. Then the Cheshire Cat's head, his paws, and tail. Urgently, as if racing against time—which, in her mind, she was—Lady Vanessa picked up speed, frantically grabbing anything that looked like it might possibly be a secret lever that would open a hidden pathway to hell.

She waddled to the edge of the mushroom cap and slowly, carefully descended. Back on firm ground, she leaned over and ran her hand under the mushroom. Foiled, she circled the statue, clutching at nodules, and then, moving left, she ran her hands all over the Mad Hatter, pulling at his nose, trying to tilt his oversized top hat.

"There must be a secret catch, a strange angle to open the way to the netherworld. Magdalena! Come and help me at once!"

Magdalena, however, was keeping her distance. She stood beside Lance, feeling a little frightened for her boss.

"Excuse me, lady," said an irritated dad. "My daughter loves the Mad Hatter and we'd like to take a picture. Can you just let her pose for a second?"

"*Just* a second?" shrieked Lady Vanessa, imagining Autumn plummeting through a corridor lined with walls of fire as so carefully detailed in Chelsea Dunning's *Eternal Journey*. "With each tick of the clock, Lance—that young man there—risks having his one true soulmate fall deep into the abyss of a loveless eternity!"

"Is this an act? Street theater?"

"How dare you! An act? Oh, this is madness. You passionless commoners will never understand! Meanwhile, your children are likely being secretly hexed and cursed and will soon be destined to meet with the hounds of hell if you let them stay here!"

When she failed to discover a portal catch on the Mad Hatter, Lady Vanessa moved behind Alice.

"Oh great," said the dad to his daughter. "Stand there and smile for me."

With Her Ladyship now at the back of the statue, Magdalena moved forward.

"Don't worry, folks!" Magdalena addressed the crowd. "Lady Vanessa will be leaving in a second. Sorry for the interruption."

But Her Ladyship was oblivious. Frowning, lines appeared on the frantic woman's forehead and her lips were pressed together as she summoned all her knowledge of time travel and epoch-hopping to focus on the matter consuming her.

"Incantations!" she declared to the bewildered crowd. "I forgot about incantations! Swearing allegiance to Lucifer and the underworld was exactly how Lucretia Wilson-Davies opened the portal in *The Hollows of High Castle.*"

At the sight of Lance, she began giving instructions.

"Once we locate it and you go inside, you will plummet into a vast chasm. Pull your body into a fetal position and think only of Autumn and the torrid passion that has compelled you to risk body and soul. The temperature will reach unfathomable, searing heights, and you will fear that your very being will be incinerated. But do not worry, complete immolation would deprive those beasts of seeing you suffer. When you arrive at the Devil's Gate just south of the River Styx, look for a cat and follow it, for cats, with their pincer claws, are the only animals the hounds of hell fear. She will lead you to Autumn."

"The hell I will," Lance muttered just loud enough for Magdalena to hear him.

"Lady Vanessa," said Magdalena, spotting two patrolmen approaching. "Let's come back later. After we meet some rich dudes, like you promised."

"Magdalena, how do you expect to find love if you won't help others find it? You are supposed to serve. To live, to serve, to love!"

"But the cops are coming."

"Let them come! I have done nothing wrong."

"That's not what these parents think."

By now Lady Vanessa had completed her circle of the statue and was by the White Rabbit.

"Ladies and gentlemen, I beg your pardon for my intrusion, but a great love affair hangs in the balance," she said loudly. "And I must do my utmost to help this brokenhearted young man find his perfect paramour and rescue her from the depths of hell."

The mother of the two French girls was talking to the two officers. Magdalena and Lance watched as she pointed toward Lady Vanessa.

"Look, I'm out of here," Lance told Magdalena. "I can't get involved with cops or the devil. So tell your nutty boss I'm not going in any portal to the underworld. Not even for Autumn."

"Shit, I don't blame you," said Magdalena. "But you know, I was thinking. I'm sure you had a good time with Autumn. And it felt real, like you was crazy in love. But my girl Yolanda, the week before she got married, she got wild on one final hookup with some dude she met at a club. I think that's what happened with Autumn. Her portal is probably a damn wedding reception."

Lance nodded and swallowed hard. "Thanks for ruining my bliss."

"No problem. Lady Vee, come on! Lance says he ain't gonna use a portal even if you find the damn thing."

"Nonsense! If he wants to heal his heart—"

"He'll find another girl, like every other dude in New York."

"Magdalena! That attitude does Lance a disservice! Lance?" Lady Vanessa searched the park. "Lance?! Where is he?"

"Excuse me, miss?" It was a police officer.

"Lance! Where are you?"

"Miss?"

"Yes? I'm looking for someone," said Her Ladyship, barely glancing at the police. "A heartbroken boy."

"We need to talk to you. Can we have your attention, please?"

"Lady Vee! Lance is gone. I told you! Listen to the police!"

"Ma'am?"

"But his journey…"

"Okay, ma'am," said the officer, grabbing Lady Vanessa by the elbow. "Please step this way."

"Excuse me, officer. What is the meaning of this?"

"You want to tell us who you are, where you live, and what you think you're doing?"

"Certainly. My name is Lady Vanessa, although the government knows me as Maxine More. I live at 688 West End Avenue. And I have been searching for a portal into the netherworld to help a young man win back his true love."

"He's gone, Lady Vee. Lance. He said for me to tell you thanks but no thanks."

Lady Vanessa grimaced. "That is heartbreaking." Then she looked up at the police officer. "That is what I *was* doing. But my quest is no more. Fair Lance has given up on love."

"What do you mean, portal to the netherworld? Like a path to hell?"

"Exactly."

"You were pushing kids out of the way so you could find it? You think it's on the statue?"

"I had a hunch. But I was unable to substantiate what seemed so obvious. But portals are tricky and there are no bigger tricksters than the hounds of hell, as you must know since you battle evildoers daily. As for the children, it was vital I should locate a portal before they would! Imagine one of those angels being sucked below!"

The officer nodded. He looked over at his partner. "You hear this?"

"Every word," said his partner, flashing a smile. "And I'm imagining you writing it up too."

The officer nodded again. "Ma'am, since you were trying to help this kid named Larry—"

"Lance! Doe-eyed. Pure of heart!"

"Yeah, Lance. And you wanted to protect the kids from falling in with Satan or something, we're going to let you go with a warning. But we could haul you in on assault charges, child endangerment, and being a public nuisance based on pushing kids around on the statue. You got that?" He looked at Lady Vanessa and Magdalena.

"One hundred percent, officer," Magdalena said. "Right, Lady Vee?"

"I am a *lady*, officer. And Magdalena is my lady-in-waiting. We are not a pair of common criminals. And if the parents of these little brats fail to see the import of my mission—and you may doubt me as well—that is their loss. But yes, your warning is acknowledged. And I regret any misunderstanding.

"Now, if you will please excuse us, a date with destiny awaits us!"

CHAPTER 6

In which our heroines discuss the finer points of museums, meet a heartbroken artist, and stage another intervention

Lady Vanessa and her lady-in-waiting, Magdalena, walked up Fifth Avenue in silence. This was a rarity for the two women. Magdalena, normally a chatterbox whose tongue, as Lady Vanessa once said, moved faster than her brain, was in a somber mood. Her boss, who could sound so smart, who lived alone in an apartment twice the size of Magdalena's parent's two-bedroom in Sunset Park, who knew everything in the world about romance, had seemingly lost her mind.

Magdalena knew Lady Vee was definitely an oddball. But she also knew her boss's heart was completely pure. Lady Vee wanted what everyone wanted: a man, a partner, a sex god, and a knight in shining armor to have and to hold and to take care of her and celebrate her—and bind two beating hearts into one. Was that too much to ask?

But the fact remained, Magdalena told herself, Lady Vee *had* lost her shit back in the park. She wished she had video-taped the whole thing. It would go viral! Magdalena would be an internet star, capturing this woman who was practically in tears looking for *a portal to hell* so she could help that hipster Lance—a guy Lady Vee had known for only five minutes.

She was willing to risk prison for the dude. Or not for that guy in particular but, in her mind, for love. *Damn*, Magdalena thought, *if I tried to explain it, people would think I'm the crazy one.*

Still, Lady Vee did have the best intentions. And that's what mattered, right? And her plans for meeting men—and finding the perfect suitor for Magdalena—sounded far more fun than the plans and schemes of her parents, who continually urged her to go to college; her *abuela*, who wanted her to become a nun; or the ideas floated by her friends in the neighborhood.

Delores wanted her to join the army. She wanted them to enlist together. ("They got thousands of guys trying to be all they can be, mami!" Delores would cackle. "And we'll help them!") Martine thought clubbing was the only way to meet guys ("Yo, that Tinder ain't nothing but a platform for lying and shit. Dudes be putting up pictures of some buff-cut cutie, and when you show up, he looks like that bald dude on *Seinfeld*.") and Iris wanted Magdalena to join her at secretarial school to become an executive assistant ("So I could meet, like, my own personal alpha male CEO!").

Magdalena liked Iris's plan the best. But it cost money to go to that school, and you had to work while you were there and work even harder until you met the CEO of your dreams, and even then, what if the CEO was already married? Damn! With Lady Vanessa, she was getting paid *and* getting an education *and* getting her nails done for free. Plus, Lady Vee was also offering a kind of dating service; she had practically promised to hook her up with a Mr. Right like Fabian. And if not him, then the bestie or close confident of the guy Lady Vee would wind up with. And for sure, he was going to be a classy dude.

Lady Vanessa was also lost in thought; a rarity, for she was also a prodigious talker. As they slowly walked north on the boulevard, she stewed over Magdalena letting Lance get away. She was peeved that he had vanished. But was that Magdalena's fault? Lady Vanessa regarded herself as a mentor to young Magdalena. Perhaps it was she who had failed to impart a sense of certitude and vision to her lady-in-waiting so that Magdalena would do whatever was required in service of romance.

True, Lady Vanessa had tried to impart her world-class knowledge of all things romantic—charm, crushes, carnality, courtship, candor, confidence, cupidity, concupiscence, covetousness, crisis, concubines, chases, chemistry, come-ons, captivation, charisma, coaxing, cajolery, conduct, culture, civility, coquettishness, contrivances, companionship, cads, comeliness and class—and that was just the Cs. But it was a large body of knowledge to absorb—bigger, even, than Magdalena herself. Perhaps, Lady Vanessa thought, she needed to remember two other Cs—calmness and composure—to help her reach Magdalena.

"I must be more patient," she told herself. "It is a bit of a shortcoming."

Then she wondered what else she was missing. She had her books, her looks, and a faithful lady-in-waiting. The only thing she lacked was…Nelson! It was tragic that despite all her womanly wiles, despite his exquisite manners and perfectly toned body, the man of her dreams seemed more interested in his poodle than in her. Perhaps she was too old for him. But never mind! She felt sure her charms would soon penetrate his obtuse male ways, and she would finally win his everlasting devotion. There was, of course, a small chance that he would prove an utter cad. But that was the risk faced by all who wager on love. Meanwhile, she could help Magdalena. She would continue trying to impart a fraction of her erotic and romantic expertise to the girl.

And this time, she would succeed. She had, it hurt to admit, failed miserably with her own daughter. Emma regarded the world of romance as some kind of fantasy land, as if the pain and happiness and dreams that filled the books on Lady Vanessa's shelves had nothing to do with reality! These were not just science fiction fantasies about worlds that don't exist, although Lady Vanessa had to admit the paranormal romances did sometimes veer ever so slightly into the realm of the implausible. These were not crime stories where people are killed on every other page, something that never happened in even the world's most deadly cities, like Baltimore or Ciudad Juarez! These were dispatches from real life of women's struggles to find safety, security, and love in the teetering, ever-changing world that was spiked with impure actors, greed, shifting alliances, and, ultimately, dramas beyond our control. *That* was real life! Hadn't poor Lance, the heartbroken young man they had just left, been evidence of love's dangerous and addictive power?

Lady Vanessa made a mental note to bring up this issue to Magdalena in a few hours when the aftershocks of terror caused by the unruly crowd in the park and the policemen had subsided.

"Damn!" said Magdalena, breaking the silence. She had literally stopped in her tracks, stunned by the impressive building that gloriously rose in front of them. "Who lives *here?*"

"No one, my dear," said Lady Vanessa. "That is the Metropolitan Museum of Art. Surely you've come here on school trips."

"Nope. Only the Natural History Museum. With the whale and the dinosaurs. In fourth grade."

"We shall have to return. Museums are excellent places to make the acquaintance of the more refined members of the male species."

"I thought that's why we were coming to the East Side."

"Yes, but the problem with the refined men who often spend time in museums is that they may be artists or writers, which of course is fine if they come from a family of means. But more likely, that will not be the case. And so, refined as they may be, they may lack certain qualities a lady requires."

"That's the same around my way. Some guy raps at you, but he ain't got no bank nowhere. So you just say, please, boyo, get the fuck out of my face."

"Magdalena!"

"Sorry, Lady Vee. My bad."

"I'm going to start deducting money from your wages if that coarse language continues."

"I'm doing way better than our early days, right? Give me time."

"What you say is true. You are making great strides, Magdalena."

"Thank you. No museum?"

"It is such a lovely day. Let us walk a bit longer and then explore the eateries and hotels of Madison Avenue, for that is where we are sure to meet men of class and means."

The two women strolled up the boulevard, admiring the buildings filled with multimillion-dollar apartments that overlooked the park. After a few blocks, they came upon a young woman working at a feverish pace to spread oil paintings against the exterior stone wall of Central Park.

"Free paintings!" she called out. "Take one, take all! They're either worth thousands or nothing at all. It's hard to know in the art market these days!"

Although she did consider herself an expert on male beauty and she enjoyed the one art history class she had taken back in college, Lady Vanessa was not particularly well-versed in the visual arts. Her aesthetic taste was best captured by the enchanting English castles and strapping dukes, lords, earls, and princes painted by the great Lorenz LaCanard, the celebrated book cover artist who distilled so many complex romance stories down to their two-dimensional essence, complete with flowing, florid titles rendered in his signature purple and white lettering.

These masterful works practically launched the career of beloved romance author Florence Worthington thanks to LaCanard's singular use of shadows and light to caress and showcase the rippling biceps and well-defined bulges in the otherwise exquisitely tailored trousers of handsome Duke Charles Thomas Rampart, the hero of Worthington's unrivaled hexalogy: *Rampart's Rise*, *Rampart's Rift*, *Rampart's Riches*, *Rampart's Ruin*, *Rampart's Return*, and *Rampart's Reign*.

Lady Vanessa peered closely at the woman's paintings, closing one eye and then the other. None of them remotely resembled LaCanard's lusty, noble works. They were, instead, an odd collection: a series of self-portraits that looked as if the woman had painted herself using a fun-house mirror, two still-lifes of lemons and glasses of lemonade, and several canvases devoted to a handsome, thin man with a sinister-looking goatee and a touch of gray in his hair being assaulted by a number of lethal-looking implements: guns, knives, swords, axes, bats, poison-tipped darts, and a cat o' nine tails.

"That's mad brutal," Magdalena said, stopping in front of the disturbing images. "Who's the guy getting dusted? Like the devil?"

"In a manner of speaking," said the artist, an odd smile pulling at the sides of her lips. "Yes, the devil."

"I knew it!"

"He's also known as a rich douchebag, a liar, a pompous poseur, and my former fiancé."

"Oh," said Magdalena, making a face. "You mean he was a dick."

"Magdalena!"

"Sorry, m'lady!"

"That is a one-dollar deduction from your salary."

"Damn."

"Two dollars."

"Sh...I mean sure."

"Now you're learning."

"Free paintings!" called the artist, moving firmly away from the two oddballs. "Take 'em, resell 'em if you can! Or paint over 'em! I couldn't care less!"

Lady Vanessa pursued the artist. "I beseech you," she said. "Hear these words: when a woman has been scorned, do not let her rain scorn down upon herself!"

"Who said that?" snorted the artist. "Woody Allen?"

"Aurora Saint Buffington to her suicidal niece Hope in *The Last Best Hope*."

"Never heard of her. What is that? A book?"

"Yes, the greatest jilted-at-the-altar epic ever written. Twice in a five-year period when Hope was in the prime of her indescribable beauty, fate's cruel winds and a wicked, miserly uncle forced her to flee down the aisle alone. Twice!"

"Well, too bad for her. Listen, I'm not running a book club here. Please take a painting and burn it."

"They are your paintings, are they not?"

"Yes. Every stinking last one of them."

"But why? Why work so hard, framing them only to then trash them? These paintings are part of you. Why ask strangers to destroy them?"

"It's a long story and too damn painful to go into," she said, dismissing Lady Vee and her sentiments and turning to face the street.

"Paint over 'em, use 'em for kindling!"

The phrase "too painful" was all the information Lady Vanessa needed to confirm her initial hunch: This woman was the victim of a cruelly broken heart! There were, of course, myriad reasons why an artist might choose to destroy his or her work: to increase the value of other paintings, or because the work is inferior, or because the artist has just been diagnosed with a terrible neurological disorder and can't cope with the prospect of vanishing talent. But this artist had just used the words "too painful" and "former fiancé," and that, to Lady Vanessa's mind, was proof positive that love—or the misfirings of love—had wounded the tortured artist before her.

"You poor thing!" she said, scrunching her face to look pained and as empathic as possible. "Whenever you are ready to share your story, Magdalena and I are here to listen and support you. I can't imagine what happened that would make you destroy all your hard work."

"Who cares if it was hard work if the actual painting was shitty? And they were all created under my fucking delusions of adequacy, never mind grandeur!"

Lady Vanessa didn't really understand the concept of delusions of adequacy, but she could see this woman was under a great deal of stress, and she was determined to be of assistance.

"Why don't we sit on the bench here or go get some tea on Madison Avenue, and you can tell me why you feel the way you feel."

"Sorry, lady. No can do. I need to watch and see if anyone will take my paintings for free."

"Why's that so important?" asked Magdalena.

"Because that will confirm what I suspected for the last three years. That I'm an awful painter. And it'll help confirm what I've suspected for the last twenty-four hours. That my fiancé is a total fraud and the world's biggest asshole!"

At these words Lady Vanessa briefly smiled and brought her hands together in what started out as a clap of glee over this confirmation that the artist's agony was indeed the aftermath of a romantic collapse and that now a tale of joy and misery would almost certainly unfold with an end that would be unspeakably sad.

But Her Ladyship realized mid-clap that glee was not the proper response to someone you wanted to convince to tell the story of their heart being torn to shreds, and so instead, she clasped her hands together and said, "Your fiancé is a fraud? What kind of fraud?"

"It's a long story," said the artist, shaking a cigarette from a pack in the front pocket of her smock. She looked exhausted and defeated.

"Well, it sounds like quite an emotional tale," said Lady Vanessa. "And I believe it might do you some good to tell it to us."

"Yes. Lady Vanessa is an expert when it comes to love stories," Magdalena coaxed.

"Who's Lady Vanessa?" asked the artist.

"Her," said Magdalena, pointing to her boss.

"Well, this is not a love story. This is a story of an awful, cruel betrayal."

"No doubt it is brutal," said Lady Vanessa. "But perhaps it is just a horrible end to a second act, and a triumphant third act awaits you!"

The artist took the cigarette out of her mouth, exhaled, and gave Lady Vanessa a blank stare as she sized up the oddly dressed woman, wondering if she was a total crank.

But Lady Vanessa looked back, her dark eyes somehow exuding sympathy that the artist took to mean Lady Vanessa was present and concerned. She had no way of knowing Her Ladyship was silently offering a prayer to the gods of love to provide her with yet another opportunity to heal a broken heart and immerse herself in the joining of two souls.

Then the artist waved them to a bench by the wall.

"You better sit down. I'll tell you if you promise not to laugh."

"You have my word as a lady," Lady Vanessa said solemnly.

"Mines too," said Magdalena.

The artist looked doubtful but decided to unburden herself anyway.

"I was sitting in a Starbucks about two years ago, just doodling on my sketchpad before my class at the Art Students League. A guy a little bit older than me, maybe thirty, sat down.

"I could feel his eyes on me, which is always annoying. I looked up. Normally, when guys try to strike up conversations in coffee shops, I make it very clear I have no interest in bonding with them. But this guy was wearing a beret that had an Obama button stuck on it and he had a warm smile, so when he asked what I was working on, I answered him. Although I hate to admit it, I probably even smiled.

"I told him I was just doodling. I love to doodle. Then I said that earlier I'd been working on a series of portraits, and I'd been drawing my own face from memory and was finding it difficult. I don't know why—probably because he was handsome and seemed interested—but I showed him some of my failed sketches.

"'I'd say you have a difficult task ahead of you,' he said.

"'What's that supposed to mean?' I said.

"'You have a soulful face,' was his answer."

"Oh, snap!" said Magdalena.

"I know, right? What the hell does that mean? I said, 'You calling me ugly?'

"And he said, 'No. Not at all. The opposite of ugly.'

"'*Soulful?*' I said. 'They don't teach soulful in portraiture.'

"'I just meant it's a—'

"I cut him off. 'How about you just quit while you're behind?' I said.

"'That's a very good idea. Thank you.'

"'You're very welcome,' I said, and put my sketchpad in my backpack and left. The next week, though, he showed up again."

"Ooh la la!" said Magdalena.

"Keep your soundtrack to yourself, Magdalena, or I shall subject you to a monetary penalty," said Lady Vanessa. "Please, carry on. No, wait. One question: What is your name?"

"Me? Alex. Alexandra. Anyway, he sat down next to me again and said he wanted to apologize for his awkward comment. And he handed me a gift-wrapped box.

"'A little something to encourage you to keep up with your portraiture,' he said. I told him it was unnecessary.

"'So is being accidentally insulted by clueless men in coffee shops,' he said.

"I liked that comment. It showed self-awareness. So I thanked him and left. I was curious to see if he'd be at the coffee shop the following week, but he didn't show up. I admit it—I was a little disappointed. I even lingered a bit longer than usual at the coffee place and arrived at my portraiture class late, which never happens.

"But after class I walked to the subway, and who should I see coming in the opposite direction? Mr. Coffeeman himself.

He seemed totally surprised and asked if he could join me for the ride. I said, 'Only if you tell me your name.'

"He said, 'You'll never believe me, but it's true: John Smith.' He even pulled out his wallet and showed me his driver's license. He told me he'd thought about getting it changed but then decided against it. 'Nobody ever forgets my name,' he said. And now that I think about it, that's unfortunately true. I'll never forget the bastard as long as I live.

"Well, one thing led to another. It seemed he was independently wealthy or maybe had a trust fund. He said he dabbled in investments."

"What? Like drugs?" asked Magdalena. "That's the word around my way. Perps be like, 'My homie is down in South Beach making some mad investments.'"

"No. Not drugs. He liked craft beers and single malt whiskey, like every other white guy in Manhattan between the ages of thirty-three and fifty. But anyway, what I mean is, he had plenty of time to spend with me, which was kind of rare in my experience.

"And I was flattered by it. Anyway, you know how it goes... we became lovers. But it was weird because I was just scraping by, studying painting and waitressing at Cleo's in Brooklyn Heights. And he'd be at my beck and call and would pay for everything—expensive meals, theater tickets, shows at the Guggenheim, a trip to Tortola.

"One day, I protested that he spent too much on me. I said, 'It's not fair. If only I could sell some of my damn paintings and live off that, then I could pay my own way.' I was just dreaming out loud.

"He told me not to worry about it. He said it would all even out in the end. And then he said he loved me. I told him I loved him too."

Here, Alex paused for a moment. There had been a slight tremble in her voice, and it was clear to Lady Vanessa that the poor woman was fighting back intense feelings of anger, sorrow, and loss.

"After that, I didn't care so much about the money. We were a serious couple. He consulted me on furniture for his apartment. We started looking at getting a bigger place, so we could live together. And then, amazingly, at the Art Students' League spring exhibition, a young gallery owner named Thatcher Gleason asked if he could represent me.

"I couldn't believe it. This was my whole dream. This was my reason for coming to this overpriced, overhyped city. To paint, mainly, but a small part of me hoped against hope that I could somehow be good and be discovered. I was over the moon and so was Mr. John Smith. He was an artist, too, it turned out. A bullshit artist.

"I signed with Thatcher Gleason. He took two paintings and sold them both in a month for five thousand dollars each. I was walking on air. Someone had bought my art. I was an artist! A painter! I called John and gushed. I called my parents and my best friend Ollie from high school.

"Over the next few months, my paintings sold steadily. Thatcher Gleason said he was shocked by how well I was doing. I asked him if he thought I was ready for my first show. He said he'd look at the calendar and see if there were others I could pair with. He didn't want me to shoulder an entire show.

"I was still waitressing, but I was down to only two shifts a week. And a month ago, John Smith proposed. I said yes, of course."

"Of course," echoed Lady Vanessa and Magdalena, thoroughly engrossed in the story.

"I started making plans to move in with him. He gave me a set of keys, not that I needed them. He was always there. But last week, he had a toothache and ran out of the house to an emergency appointment. I was lounging around, sleeping in, daydreaming about my future, when the phone rang.

"I was John's fiancée, but I didn't think I should answer his phone. It didn't seem right. I'd never met his family, although he was making plans for us to visit them in LA. I let the answering machine take the call. I'd never even had a landline in my five years in New York, so when the call picked up, I was smiling to myself, trying to remember how long it had been since I last used an answering machine.

"The machine gave it's 'leave a message' beep, and then I heard a man's voice:

"'*John, it's Tony. I just got the picture from the gallery, but my sister is coming to town and I need the room. It's getting a little crowded in there, with like, twelve paintings, and you know, family! Maybe get a storage space? Call me back.*'

"That smile I had? It vanished. Nausea swept over me. I fought it off, but now I wished I'd puked all over his apartment. Tony was a friend of John's college buddy Ray Forsyth. I didn't know much about him, except he ran a poker game every other Thursday night. Now, thanks to the message, I knew he'd been storing pictures from a gallery for John!

"And you know what? John never said a word to me about buying any paintings. Never once! I tried to tell myself it wasn't what I thought. That he was going to surprise me with this fantastic collection he'd secretly amassed. It would be his gift, a wedding present to me.

"But I knew that didn't add up. Because Tony said twelve paintings. And that was the exact number of paintings I'd sold. I could do that math. I knew who my mystery buyer was. John fucking Smith.

"I fled the apartment. I went to stay with Nancy, a friend from the restaurant. I was a mess. I am a mess. I feel like a goddamn Jackson Pollack painting. My mind is just splattered. I'm ready to kill that fucker."

Alex turned away and lit another cigarette, then stood up and walked back to her display.

"Free paintings! Take one, take 'em all! The artist sold one of her works for twelve thousand dollars! Have at it!"

"Please," said Lady Vanessa. "My heart is torn in half! But it will be sheared into quarters and then eighths if you do not find John Smith and reconcile!"

"Reconcile! Me?! That bastard conned me! Deluded me!"

"He wanted to make you happy!"

"Bullshit! He thought I was his plaything."

"Oh dear," said Lady Vanessa, who knew Alex was not wrong. "That may be true. And you can and should feel total betrayal. But it does not discount what I have said. Two opposite things can both be true! He did deceive you, but he did it to make you happy. Even if you are now miserable."

Now it was Alex's turn to pause, but she covered her hesitation—her momentary consideration of Lady Vanessa's point that John Smith, in some misguided, clueless way, thought he was helping her—by lighting another cigarette. Then she said, "How could he think living a lie would make me happy?"

"When you thought it was true," asked Magdalena, "were you happy?"

"Yes! Yes, of course. I told you, I was over the moon. I was over Jupiter!"

"Then what he did made you happy."

"Thank you, Magdalena," said Lady Vanessa. "You are making an old woman proud."

"You ain't that old, Lady Vee. My mama's older than you."

Alex took a huge drag on her cigarette. She bit her lip. She was shaking with fury. "I was happy. It's true. And now look at me! Who would *do* something like that?"

"Alex, there is nothing to fathom. He was simply delirious with love for you. It drove him crazy, that love. You were his world. No, you were the axis on which his world turned! And I tell you, my poor, broken little bird, if he sees you, he will understand at once what his madness has done and be forever beholden to you to do all that is good and true. For he has wounded you unforgivably and yet will never stop loving you and grieving for you, all because of the pain his madness has caused."

Alex marched up to a self-portrait, lay it flat on the ground, lifted her foot up, and stomped heel-first through the canvas. As she approached the second, Magdalena sprang up and grabbed Alex by her arms.

"No, no!" she said. "I want that one."

"Don't humor me! And let me go! You're violating my free speech!"

Magdalena swung Alex's arms away in disgust. "I was holding your arms, not your tongue!"

"Magdalena!" cried Lady Vanessa. "Let her smash them all if she wants. She's been driven mad. Anyone can see her agony! This is a dangerous weapon we are witnessing. The explosive passion of two perfectly matched souls clashing."

Alex grabbed another portrait, raised it high in the air, rushed toward Lady Vanessa, and smashed it down on Her Ladyship's head.

Lady Vanessa's cranium broke through the thick canvas and the frame rested on her shoulders. But she didn't notice.

She had been knocked unconscious.

TRANSLATOR'S NOTE #4

Although it is a stylistic break in both voice and format, the upcoming interlude appears, evidently written in the first person by the mysterious author Aisha Benengeli. I have reproduced it here faithfully, even though it is a bit of intensely personal commentary that does not truly factor into the narrative of our titular heroine. But Benengeli strikes me as a master puppeteer, and I feel obligated to document her original manuscript and the strings she has chosen to pull. Indeed, who am I to reject such a singular talent?

CHAPTER 7

In which a new character introduces herself

And so, dear reader, I am at a sinister, writerly crossroads.

When a character, especially a major character, is knocked unconscious, the writer is instantly presented with an opportunity to make a narrative leap so grand, it may seem as if it was launched from a trampoline or with the help of a vaulting pole. I have now presented myself with this opportunity. But should I, Aisha Benengeli, take it?

This is an extremely important and perplexing question. I'm not complaining. Or maybe I am. Every page, every sentence, every clause, I am faced with choices, with crossroads. The heroine enters a room. Is there a mirror on the wall? Yes? Should she look into it? What does she see? Should she scream in horror at the sight of her hollow, sockets-only, pupil-less eyes? Or be charmed by the true beauty she never realized she had?

So you see, I'm making choices all the time. But getting knocked unconscious! That's right up there with a man walking into a room with a gun. What then?

React?

Or stay calm?

Or pull out your own gun?

Or throw your scalding hot coffee in the gunman's face and run for it?

You can see why, sitting here in my air-conditioned suite at the Four Seasons Hotel in San Stefano, Alexandria, I am sweating. Some brilliant writers would waste not a second and thrust our heroine into a complex new storyline. While she's unconscious, an old lover, a man wounded in Iraq, walks by and recognizes her! Hearing his voice, she awakens, and thus begins a torrid affair. Should I do that? Or maybe he should fall in love with Magdalena. Should I do that?

Or perhaps I should use this idea of the knockout in a different story altogether and go back and have Lady Vanessa dodge the frame. Then I could write a completely different story: During a war, a woman takes a new lover after giving up her old lover, a soldier at the front, for dead. She is knocked out during a bombing and falls into a coma. But then it turns out her old lover is alive! He returns from the front and discovers the new lover at her bedside. As if that's not bad enough, he learns his entire family was killed the previous winter after a septic tank exploded and the roof collapsed, caving in on his elderly mother, three sisters, and cat. Despondent, the old lover pulls out a gun, but just before he can pull the trigger, the woman awakens and cries out, "No!"

That would be something!

But would it be *the right* something?

Other talents, other writers with skills and experience far, far greater than mine, might opt for a completely different scenario. Perhaps a completely different drama should play out around our comatose, love-obsessed, middle-aged train wreck. What if she doesn't wake up and an ambulance is called? She is rushed to the hospital: The doctor, a nerdy loner who cares for our heroine, falls in love with her. He sees her struggles, her beating heart, her constantly oxygenating blood, and he is enamored beyond the beyond. Where others see pale, wan skin, he sees a translucent glow. Where some might worry about her gaunt physique, he sees a body determined to use all its resources to go on, to live, to love!

Actually, that story would get really annoying. Even sickening. What creep that doctor is, falling in love with a vegetable when there are so many other wonderful, full-brained, full-bodied women out there. He's so crazy, he hatches a plan to steal her body from the hospital, reanimate her, and turn her into a love slave whom he dresses in plush. Luckily, a good man, a Christian man who works in hospital security, stops the sicko doctor as he's stowing our gal in an ambulance. In the penultimate scene, the two men beat the crap out of each other (I'm paraphrasing) and in the hurly-burly, the rough and tumble, the fierce fisticuffs, the lady's oxygen machine is disconnected. The cardio monitor has a brief flatline, and the resulting *beeeeeep* of death stops the two men for a brief second, allowing the security guy to finally bash the doctor's head in. Suddenly, the *beeeeeeeeep* stops and gets its rhythm back: beep, beep, beep, beep. And glory be! Saints alive! *In'shallah!* Lady Vanessa is opening her eyes...on the handsome man who saved her from becoming a sex slave to a demented doctor!

Whatever the storyline I come up with here, the real problem is the resolution. Put another way: to dream or not to dream, that is the question for an author when a character is knocked unconscious. I could spin all the aforementioned scenarios and smoothly abandon them with but a scant four words: then she woke up. Or, in an old-timey book, three words: then she awakened. Or maybe, "then she awoke." I'm never sure. Ah, yet another choice to make.

But I absolutely hate listening to dreams in real life, so why should I resort to this ancient plot device now? I wrote a short story once that used a dream. It was the only time I was ever tempted by such a ruse. This is how it began: *One night, Amanda Green dreamed she was masturbating to online porn videos. When she woke up, she realized she had become sexually aroused during her dream state, and she grew depressed because she realized she had become excited by dreaming that she was watching others having sex, not having it herself. Her arousal was at the idea of watching pornography, not having sex. This was a distressing thought. The internet was killing everything. It wasn't enough that it had exploded the economy with bubble stocks; stripped the world of so many office and manual labor jobs, from accounting to answering the phone to filing; destroyed the publishing and newspaper industries, and screwed over the music industry. Now it was ruining Amanda's erotic dreams. And she thought, for the first time ever, about killing herself.*

That is the only time I have ever written about a dream. A dream that didn't live up to the potential of dreams, which, really, is every dream ever when you think about it because a dream is often thought of and articulated as a state of perfection. Of bliss. And yet dreams lack the linear, cartesian logic that I identify with a perfect story. There are messy jump cuts. A lack of internal logic. The plotting is uneven, the characterizations often completely without depth. The problem with my short story was that the setup made too much sense. It had too much logic. It was too clear and not dreamy enough for me. So right away, I felt the whole thing was ruined. Part of me hates dreams. And 'now, awake in my air-conditioned suite in a luxe hotel, provided by my rich, deceitful husband, I am no closer to perfection, to truly living the dream, than anyone.

Oh, sure, I'm lucky! I have no concerns about money, food, or clothes, and no stress about kids, since, as a late-to-the-altar couple, we don't have any. But as a writer, there is only work. Only choices. Only questions: Am I good enough? Am I serving my character, my reader, myself? Will anyone possibly care about my work? Will they see the humor? Or will they be offended? Will they dismiss me as a rip-off artist, who has simply and disrespectfully raided the pages of an epic work and violated it, like some literary cat burglar who purloins a Picasso and then slices and dices the elements of the picture into a collage Scotch-taped to a bathroom wall. Maybe I should burn these pages right here in the shadow of the Library of Alexandria, where all great books once lived—Africa's pre-Google paradise of knowledge!—before a disastrous fire reduced all its books to ash. And now we live in a world where certain books—eBooks—cannot even be reduced to ash because they don't physically exist. How is it that I am toiling in a craft where the final product is air? Or to be charitable, zeroes and ones. But I don't have the answer. I'm just driven. Despite the fact these words only exist on a computer until I print them. Despite the fact that, if I am even modestly successful despite my obvious shortcomings—the pathetic jokes and implausible scenarios, the overt manipulations and limited vocabulary, and the relentless satire that hammers and hammers and hammers at a beloved genre while also, arguably, celebrating the form—a shrewd strategy that will, I hope and pray, render me unassailable to critics and literary know-it-alls of all stripes. They will doubtlessly aim poisoned arrows at some or all of the aforementioned, not least of all comparing me to the inconceivable, unmatchable genius of Miguel de Cervantes, a madman, adventurer, and maestro, unrivaled by all who have dared pick up pen and paper in his wake, who invented postmodern fiction just as the novel was being born. Even if I succeed in having my work published, I will likely be a failure—ignored by booksellers and book buyers and humiliated by readers who deem me a charlatan, clown, and plagiarist and who, worst of all, hate my creation.

So excuse my pause, dear reader, at this most tense time, with Lady Vanessa unconscious, possibly gravely injured, or lost to a dream state. I wanted to evaluate my options. When you are an amateur author with no credentials beyond a liberal arts education at a semi-elite American college and a sheltered adolescence as a diplomat's daughter who briefly read bodice-rippers without, initially, knowing what a bodice was, you may have a storytelling quandary or two.

And yes, sometimes you stall for time.

But that is over now.

CHAPTER 8

In which bleary, leery Lady Vanessa meets John Smith and disaster looms

With the large face of Magdalena and the smaller, more finely shaped visage of Alex looming over her, Lady Vanessa opened her eyes. The portrait braining had knocked her out for five fright-filled seconds. Not fright-filled for her, naturally, because she was unconscious, but for poor Magdalena and Alex, who leapt up and stood stunned over her prone body until she mercifully opened her eyes.

As Lady Vanessa regained her senses, lying on the cobblestone sidewalk outside the park, her head and shoulders jutting through the canvas, she was understandably quite groggy. Alex's profuse apologies gave her time to catch her bearings.

"I am so, so sorry, Lady Vanessa!" Alex said, crouching beside her victim. "I don't know what came over me. I was just so enraged at the idea of anyone defending John Smith! He gaslighted me! Are you okay?"

"Yo, Lady Vee," said Magdalena calmly, as she could see at a glance Her Ladyship was fine. "Repeat after me: Fabio, Mr. Darcy, safe word, bling, and foreplay."

"Why?"

"Just do it. It's a test."

"Fabio, Mr. Darcy, safe word, bling, and foreplay."

"She's okay. She's good."

"How do you know?" asked Alex. "Are you a nurse?"

"My dad watches football. He told me about the concussion test. If Lady Vee couldn't remember any of that, we'd have to take her to the hospital."

"I'm fine!" said Lady Vanessa, ducking her head back out of the portrait and raising the frame above her head. "Just get this thing off me."

"I am so, so, so sorry!" said Alex again, grabbing the frame and tossing it. "I've never done anything like that before. But when you said that shit about perfectly matched souls, I just lost it."

"Yes. The truth hurts. But it is my duty as an expert in all coronary matters and passion-fueled disputes to tell you the larger truth."

"How can we be matched?! I want to *kill* the scumbag bastard!"

"You feel that way now. But if you sever your relationship, in six months you will see the error of your ways."

"Six months?" said Magdalena, disbelief in her voice. "How old are you?"

"Thirty-three," said Alex.

"It won't take that long, Lady Vee. She just needs an hour on Tinder to remind her of her future! Ain't nobody there going to spend bank on you like this guy! Damn!"

"I'm not thinking about money!"

"Nor am I," said Lady Vanessa. "And to be quite honest, I don't think John Smith cared about the money, either. He cared about you. He cared about making you happy, about making you feel fulfilled. He wants to marry you."

"Well, then he should have married me as a loser painter!"

"I daresay he will, if you let him."

"No. Fucking. Way."

"Very well. Magdalena, call the police."

"What?"

"If Alex will not at least meet with John Smith, I must press assault charges against her."

"You're blackmailing me?"

"I'm *saving* you."

"Don't call the cops," said Alex, her hands shaking as she lit another cigarette. "You're right. I'll meet John. I know just what I'll tell him, too."

"And what would that be?"

But Alex didn't respond. As if on cue, a taxicab pulled up at the corner. The three women watched as an impeccably dressed, handsome man got out of the car. "Alex!" he called. "I've been looking for you for two days!"

The man rushed toward Alex, and Lady Vanessa knew at once that this was John Smith. He had bags of fatigue and stress below his steel-grey eyes. His skin was tanned, his features were perfectly symmetrical, and his black hair was going gray at the temples. He looked, in Lady Vanessa's estimation, like a worn-out primetime TV stud who had just spent the last two days saving New York from certain annihilation.

Alex grabbed another painting and held it up like a shield. "Stay the fuck away from me."

"Alex, what happened? Where have you been? No text, no note, your phone isn't even on!" He looked at the arrangement of artwork. "What's with the paintings?"

"I should ask you the same question. You want to know where I've been? You want to know why I didn't respond? Go home and listen to your goddamn answering machine!"

John Smith stared at his fiancée. Then he said, "Oh, shit. Tony. You heard that?"

"Of course I fucking heard that. I never want to see you again."

"Oh, honey, listen to me. I screwed up. As soon as I bought the first two paintings, I realized I'd screwed up. But I'd done it. I never even planned to do it, I swear. It was spur of the moment."

"Bullshit. I bet you got the gallery to take me on too. Did you pay for that?"

"I convinced them to show the paintings, but I did not pay them! Everyone needs a break. You could have all the talent in the world, but if you don't have luck or the right connections, you're screwed. That goes for *all* the arts—writing, music, theater. When I invited him to see your stuff, I never intended to buy twelve paintings. I never even intended to buy one! But when I saw how proud you were to have them hanging on the gallery wall...how unspeakably happy you were...it made me happy.

"I went back two days later, and I got worried. What if they didn't sell? Would that rob you of your joy, your pride? I couldn't bear it. I called the gallery and bought them anonymously. As soon as I hung up the phone, I thought, 'John, what the hell did you just do?'

"And then it steam-rolled. You got happier and more confident with each sale. Your painting got better too. Thatcher at the gallery even said so. He says the new work is getting more interest. Call him right now—he'll tell you."

"Did he know you bought my paintings?"

"No. I paid by bank checks, and I had Tony pick them up."

"Thatcher is a piece of shit too!"

"I can see how you think that. But gosh, I'm so glad you're okay! I was so worried."

"I'm not okay! Do I seem okay to you?"

"Well, you're smoking and shaking, so no. But you're alive! You have no idea the kind of crazy shit you can think up, especially when the dentist gives you Percocet."

"Please leave."

"What? Because of the paintings? C'mon! Alex! I screwed up. Big time. I was a dick. I did one very, very stupid thing. But you *have* to forgive me."

At this, Lady Vanessa could no longer keep silent.

"She does not have to forgive you, John Smith! You have to *earn* forgiveness!"

"Excuse me? Who are you?"

"Who I am is not important, although I am known and admired far and wide as Lady Vanessa of Manhattanshire, a woman who possesses equal parts beauty and brains as well as one hundred percent extra-virgin seductive powers.

"No, what is important is that you work eternally to reap the glory of Alex's trust. This is not a one-day boo-boo to which your beloved can apply a psychic bandage. You have rattled her sense of self and her trust in you, the man she thought she wanted to marry. These are grave shortcomings. You must accept them and atone. And give her time."

"Um, excuse me, but did I ask for your advice?"

"Shut up, John. She may look crazy. But she just spoke like a mind reader."

"Really? You think we're over?"

"Right now, I never want to see you again, you fucking douchebag!"

"But—"

Lady Vanessa cut him off. "I believe, based on the sincerity of your ultimate motives—making Alex happy—that you do, in fact, love her deeply. And I have counseled Alex to give your relationship time. Now, Magdalena, shall we take one of these fine self-portraits and go?"

"Okay, Lady Vee. Let's take this one. Look how happy she is here!"

"Yes. A very good choice."

"Please don't leave me alone with him!" Alex implored the two women.

"Alex, you are not alone. And John Smith will bother you no more today. He will give you space. I am sure of it."

"I'll leave," said Smith, looking despondent. "But hear me, Alex! I love you. And every cell in my body is filled with regret. I'm begging you. Please give me a chance to make this right."

Alex lit another cigarette. She glanced briefly at her ex, who leaped at the gesture.

"Thank you," John Smith said to Alex. "I know I can make this up to you." He turned to the crazy-looking woman who seemed to believe in him. "And thank you, Lady Vanessa."

"You have caused a great deal of pain," Lady Vanessa intoned. "But perhaps it will have been worth it if, in some small way, I have helped push you toward a more perfect union. Now go and give your true love the space she needs to heal."

"What Lady Vee said!" chimed Magdalena.

They watched John Smith hail a cab, get in and offer a solemn wave through the backseat window.

Lady Vanessa took the portrait Magdalena had selected. "Alex, you look radiant in this picture," she said. "And I believe if you both put in the work to communicate, this glow of happiness will return."

"Hard to imagine."

"John Smith is not the first man to think his money can buy happiness for his beloved. I believe you have taught him an important lesson. Now, Magdalena and I have our own rich men to meet, truth be told. But we don't want to leave you here alone."

"No. I'm okay. I still want to get rid of these pictures. I'm going to take up sculpture and work with a hammer and chisel and a torch. Nobody will mess with me then!"

"How can we check on you?"

"You don't need to do that. I can take care of myself."

Lady Vanessa took a pen and a small notebook out of her bag. "Here is my number," she said. "If you need support, do not hesitate to call. But good luck. I believe that man loves you very much, and that, my friend, is half the battle."

CHAPTER 9

In which Lady Vanessa and Magdalena lure two mad men on a bacchanal

It was nearing 4 p.m. when Lady Vanessa led her charge east across Fifth Avenue toward Madison.

As they arrived and turned left, Magdalena spied the street sign and said, "So this is, like, where the *Mad Men* come from."

"What are you talking about?"

"The TV show? *Mad Men?* It's a show about advertising and martinis, yo. It was mega-hot and popular."

"Those types of firms are farther downtown. This is a more residential neighborhood. There are some very fine shopping emporia up here, as well as art dealers, antique dealers, and fine hotels."

"Yeah. I can see that. So where are all the sugar daddies?"

"If by 'sugar daddies' you mean wealthy males willing to spend money on women, that is a good question. Many of them stay at home and have their chefs prepare meals."

"Chefs? In their apartments?"

"Yes, dear. I told you. This is New York's land of plenty."

"Not Wall Street?"

"That is the daytime land of plenty. They all come up here to sleep. Or travel to their homes in Greenwich, Connecticut."

"Damn man, imagine having two different cribs!"

"If by 'cribs,' you mean homes—really Magdalena, we must start working on your vocabulary choices—two is understating the case, my dear."

"For, like, everybody?"

"No, certainly not, Magdalena. Not every man you feast your eyes on is going to be scion or powerbroker."

Maggie had no idea what a scion was, and this provoked a momentary swirl of self-doubt. "Maybe we should just go home," she said. "We've had two amazing adventures. A third one might just give us a heart attack."

"Absolutely not!" declared Lady Vanessa. "At the very least, we must explore New York's most important boulevards—the arteries of affluence and the promenades of prosperity—Madison and its even richer cousin Park Avenue, and we will sit for a cup of overpriced tea!"

"Or Arizona Iced Tea, boss."

"I'm not sure they will carry that vintage, Magdalena, but we can ask."

On the corner of Madison and 81st, a bell captain greeted them by doffing his cap.

"I love a man in a uniform," whispered Magdalena.

"We all do," nodded Lady Vanessa. "Except for insolent police threatening to arrest you."

"Don't worry, Lady Vee. You ain't black or Dominican. Those cops was gonna let you slide."

"I must admit, I am rather proud I kept my equanimity during that exchange."

"Yes, and you didn't panic or get stressed, either."

"That's what keeping equanimity means."

"Oh, sorry."

"Don't worry. You will improve under my tutelage. You already have! Look, let's turn around and go to that hotel. I am exhausted, and the doorman was quite handsome."

The women reversed their steps and were rewarded by a buoyant greeting. "Welcome, ladies," said the doorman, every golden tassel in his epaulets glimmering.

"Thank you, sir," said Lady Vanessa. "We require some refreshment. Some beverages."

"Our Cafe Yellow is just inside to the right," he said, offering a slight bow.

The two women walked through the reception area, an airy, mirrored lobby with sofas set at angles that invited conversation.

Cafe Yellow had a predictable color scheme, and although Lady Vanessa admired it, sensing it was a refined establishment for travelers of a certain income, age, and sensibility, a place for art lovers who wanted to be near the esteemed Museum Mile and for shoppers who came to study the glorious ABCs of the area—Armani, Baccarat, and Cartier—it was not the right venue for her purpose.

It was a cafe designed to appeal to women. And as such there were no men on the premises, nor, likely, would there be. "Excuse me," she asked the waitress who greeted her, "is there a hotel bar?"

"There's a cigar bar on the other side of reception."

"Excellent. Come along, Magdalena."

"But you hate smokers."

"I hate cigarette smoke. The aroma of a freshly clipped Macanudo is another matter."

"Is that like a Phillies Blunt? Cause that's the only cigar I know. And it gets, like, doctored up."

"A Phillies Blunt?" asked Lady Vee. "What do you mean, 'doctored up?'"

"Boys round my way cut the cigar open and stuff it with herb. You know, the four-twenty."

"Herb? Four-twenty?"

"You know, marijuana. Pot. Damn!"

"Oh! I'm sorry, Magdalena. It's just that sometimes it seems you are speaking a different language."

"It works both ways, Lady Vee. But I got you."

The women were now standing beside the heavy doors of the East Sider Cigar Club. And Lady Vanessa felt, finally, a moment of triumph. On the other side of the door would be nothing but gentlemen, wealthy men with decorum and garments that stank of tobacco; a small price to pay in the search for companionship. They might not find Mr. Right here this evening. But at least Magdalena would see her lady knew the lay of the land.

She pushed open the door and a world of dark wood and men in business suits appeared before them. The two women stepped toward the bar, between two groups of puffing males.

Immediately, one of the puffers, a tall, heavy-set fellow with gray hair, stepped toward the newcomers.

"This is a rare sight!" said the man with a notable Texan drawl. "I've been coming here all week, and y'all are two of the few ladies I've seen brighten this place up. May I have the pleasure of buying you both a drink?"

"Thank you," said Lady Vanessa with a gracious smile. "That would be most welcome and gallant. I shall have a gin and tonic."

"Excellent choice. And you?"

"Arizona Iced Tea, please. Large."

"We don't have that," said the barman. "But I make a mean Long Island iced tea."

"I'll try that."

"It's not a regular iced tea," Lady Vanessa told her charge.

"I know. It's, like, from Long Island."

"*Hahaha!*" roared the Texan. "You're a funny one, ain't ya!"

"That's true. I always like my lady-in-waiting to have wit in addition to charm."

"Lady-in-waiting! Are you royalty? Gentlemen!" he called to his fellow cigar aficionados. "We have a princess in our midst."

"I am not a princess!"

"No, she's a lady. This is Lady Vee, y'all," said Magdalena, who noticed her boss flashing a face of distaste and realized her mistake. "I mean, Lady Vanessa. Of Manhattanshire. And I am her lady-in-waiting, Magdalena Cruz."

"Here are your drinks," said the barman.

"Thank you," Lady Vanessa said. "You are a mixologist of unrivaled speed."

"You're welcome, m'lady."

Then she turned to the man who ordered the drinks. "And thank you, sir. Do you have a name?

"I am Wynton C. Tapworth of the Houston Tapworths."

"We are very pleased to make your acquaintance," said Lady Vanessa, wondering if he was in oil or silver or finance. "What brings you to our city?"

"The fast-food convention at the Javits Center. Although I prefer to do business here."

"Fast-food convention! Damn! Is that like all you can eat?" asked Magdalena. "I'd never leave."

"*Hahaha!*" roared the Texan again. "There you go again!"

Lady Vanessa made a mental note to talk to Magdalena about tempering her enthusiasm regarding her passion for junk food. She realized her charge was just, in her words, "keeping it real," and that censoring her was in some way wrong. But it was also, she knew, completely right. The world was a judgmental place, and Magdalena needed to prepare herself for it.

"Lionel," Wynton C. Tapworth called to the bartender, "another round for me and the ladies."

"Damn! This iced tea is mad good," said Magdalena, sucking on the ice cubes in her otherwise empty glass.

"A convention is a convention is a convention. I'm sick of 'em! Franchise seminars, soda delivery systems, canola oil studies, cashier sciences, optimize this, automate that, digitize the other, social media twenty-four-seven. I just go from ten in the morning to one in the afternoon, rah-rah the team at the booth, talk to the home office, and get the hell out of there. My lieutenants will report to me back at home."

"What do you do after that then?"

"Meetings, lunches, dinners, cigars! When you're the third biggest franchise owner in the great state of Texas, everyone wants to sell you something."

"That sounds like a good problem to have."

"Ah! Do I sound bitter? Not at all, not at all. I just have a bad case of convention-itis."

Another man, even taller than Wynton C. Tapworth, had been listening in, hovering on the edge of the conversation. And upon hearing this last remark, he burst out laughing and slapped Tapworth on the back.

"Convention-itis! You should have come down with that three divorces ago, Wynton!" he said.

Tapworth grinned at him. "You've got that right, Davis. But no need to bore these ladies with the grave miscalculations of my personal life."

"You sound like a good businessman," said Lady Vanessa. "How is it you have thrived in business but not in matters of the heart?"

"Oh, Wynton thrived alright!" said his friend between gusts of laughter. "He thrived all the way to divorce court."

"Actually, Davis, I've never been to divorce court. That's what lawyers are for. Oh, I forgot, you were a lawyer once. So you probably knew that."

"I was just using it as a figure of speech!" boomed Davis. "Conventions are one of the top ten causes of divorce in America. You could look it up."

"How come you ain't a lawyer no more?" asked Magdalena.

"He got disbarred!" howled Wynton, as if his friend's misfortune was the funniest thing in the world. "That's when other lawyers divorce your sorry ass from the legal profession for being a crook."

"It is a matter of debate as to precisely why I was banished from my previous calling," said Davis, addressing Lady Vanessa and Magdalena. "What is not a matter of debate, however, is whether you two ladies would like to accompany us to dinner. I hear a steak calling my name."

The invitation put Lady Vanessa in a quandary. She had succeeded in introducing Magdalena to two apparently wealthy men, neither of whom were wearing a wedding band.

But both of these men were clearly over-aged cads. As such, Lady Vanessa knew she should not waste another minute of her time with them. They laughed about divorce as if marriage was nothing more than a careless trifle, a promise made with your fingers crossed behind your back. They seemed somewhat courtly and charming, however, and clearly oozed wealth.

"Ooh," said Magdalena. "I love steak!"

"Well, then, lady-in-waiting, we await your lady—"

"Lady Vee, let's go. I'm starving!"

"We shall be delighted to accept your dinner invitation. However, you must please excuse Magdalena and me for a moment while we repair to the powder room. Come along, Magdalena, at once!"

In the bathroom, Lady Vanessa gave her charge instructions.

"We are going, I imagine, to a very expensive steakhouse. You must order your food with restraint and decorum. One steak, one side dish, one vegetable. That is all. Do you understand? Do not ask for onion rings and/or French fries. Do not order mozzarella sticks, calamari, or chicken wings as a starter. You must eat with suppressed lust. Try, as I have asked before, to chew each morsel twenty times before swallowing it. And do it with your mouth closed. Taste your food. Enjoy it. And for god's sake, do not, do not, *do not* slather your steak with ketchup unless our dates—I mean, these gentlemen—do."

Magdalena, feeling loving and lightheaded from her two cocktails, smiled and nodded. Normally, Lady Vanessa's instructions would have wounded her, but now she was too drunk to care.

"I can't believe we're going!" she said, giving Lady Vanessa an impulsive hug. "I thought for sure you would say no way. These guys are just sixty-year-old has-beens with too much bank. They're like alpha males that morphed into zeta males, you know what I'm saying?"

"What did I just ask you to do?"

"No ketchup. No onion rings."

"And you agree?"

"Yes. What about dessert?"

"Absolutely not."

"Lady Vee!"

"Or we can just go home now."

"You win, boss."

"And no more Long Island iced teas. You may have one glass of wine."

"Okay. Wine is nice. Chablis. I always liked the sound of that."

"Let them order the wine. *Always* let a gentleman order the wine."

"Okay."

"No matter what happens, Magdalena, we must always protect our virtue. For without it, we are nothing to these men. Especially *these* kind of men. Give it to them, and they will abuse our gifts. Withhold it, and you shall have them exactly where you want them."

"What if what I want is for them to take my virtue?"

"Magdalena!"

"I'm just being real, Lady Vee."

"Real? These are not things a true lady or lady-in-waiting would ever say...although Portia de Randee's heroine, Moravia, in *Waiting for the Wanton Duke* certainly does *think* these things. But she keeps her carnal desires to herself until she is absolutely sure of her transcendent connection to the Duke of Devon-Upon-Shire."

"Well, you brought it up. It must be on your mind. These dudes are old enough to be my grandfathers, LOL! So ain't no serious connection gonna happen for me unless they give me diamonds, pearls, and a 401k. And have an ambulance on call!"

"I'll thank you not to drag my mind down to your gutter-level fantasies. Now, you have lipstick on your teeth. It is most unbecoming."

Soon a limousine was summoned, and the unlikely quartet was transported to Gaspari's All-American Steakhouse, with Davis in the front seat and Wynton sandwiched in the back between Vanessa and Magdalena.

The ride was punctuated by Magdalena's comments of amazement. After expressing her wonder at the fact that the driver opened the door for her and at the expansive legroom in the back seat, she declared, "Damn, this is some real-ass Kardashian shit! I'm, like, in a limo!"

"Surely, as a lady-in-waiting, you've ridden in limousines before," said Wynton.

Lady Vanessa answered. "I'm not sure. You see, Magdalena only started in my service relatively recently."

Magdalena was just about to interject that she'd been working with Lady Vee for at least four months, when Wynton cut her off.

"That explains her wonderment. It's very refreshing," he said, slapping his hands down on both Magdalena and Lady Vanessa's thighs.

"Almost as refreshing as not being groped in the backseat by a strange man," said Lady Vanessa dryly.

Wynton withdrew his hand from Lady Vee's thigh. "Oh, come now! That was just a jovial tap. Not a grope at all. You'll know a grope when I give one, I can assure you."

Meanwhile, his right hand squeezed Magdalena's thigh harder.

From the front seat, Davis laughed. "Wynton, it sounds like you're getting a mild attack of convention-itis."

"Can you blame me, sitting among such striking royalty? How is it you ladies reside in New York and not London?"

"Oh, it's a long and tiresome story. I am a divorcee. And sometimes, when one's heart has been betrayed, moving to a dazzling new locale can be good therapy."

"I'm very glad to hear that," said Wynton, his fingers now pressing against Magdalena's inner thigh.

"He means glad you're divorced," translated Davis. "Right, Wynton?"

"Yes, yes, certainly! I mean, I'm sorry things didn't work out for you, but like my pappy used to tell me, 'One man's loss is another man's game'—I mean, 'gain!' Ha ha!"

"That is so alpha, right, Lady Vee?" Magdalena asked.

"Not entirely, I'm afraid," Lady Vanessa told her charge. "For a true, worthy alpha would never rejoice in another's loss."

The limo had arrived outside the steakhouse and the chauffeur quickly launched himself out of the car to open doors. The hand on Magdalena's thigh released itself. Lady Vanessa resolved to sit next to Wynton of the wandering hands during dinner. She whispered one last word of advice to her lady-in-waiting: "Try to act like you've been to places like this before."

The dinner had gone exceedingly well, Lady Vanessa thought. The conversation was silly. The gentlemen liked to tell jokes, and she and Magdalena provided a good audience.

Lady Vanessa had only had to remove Wynton's hand from her thigh three times and once when it was draped over her shoulder.

Given that Magdalena was sitting safely opposite wanton Wynton and that Davis, who was seated next to her, did not seem quite as afflicted by convention-itis as his friend, Her Ladyship felt confident there would be minimal drama when it came time to bid these suitors good night.

She had no idea, however, that the soused franchise magnate at her side had slipped his foot out of his loafer and spent the entire meal playing footsie with Magdalena's size fourteens. The under-the-table dalliance was a unique experience for Magdalena. Groping, full-on bodily assaults, offers of money and drugs in exchange for a blowjob—these were the come-ons she was used to from Sunset Park suitors.

A man's expensively socked foot grazing her calf, his toes wedging themselves into the crook of her knee or just rubbing against her foot? This was new and weird. Some of it she liked. The physical contact was okay. Some of it made her ticklish. Some of it was distracting, like when she was trying to read the menu. She had never dined at such an expensive venue, and when she saw the prices for a New York strip, T-bone, or a porterhouse, she held the menu just inches from her face to make sure her Long Island iced tea-addled eyes weren't playing tricks on her. Seventy dollars for a single steak? She felt completely out of her league. What were these guys playing at? That would feed her whole family for two days at Popeyes Chicken or provide a week of Happy Meals.

Meanwhile, Lady Vanessa struggled to keep her composure. On one hand, she was thrilled that her plans to meet men of the world had panned out and that she had succeeded in showing Magdalena another side of New York, of the upper class, of opportunity. On the other, these men were geriatric cads, and she worried about ending the evening without insulting them or weakening and falling for their wiles.

She had warmed to Davis's solicitous behavior. Unlike the pawing, leering Wynton, he was polite and even charming. He was handsome in a patrician manner. He looked like Allen J. Crumbwell, the elderly heartthrob of Darla Demimonde's *Attorney at Love*. But she sensed he was a different kind of snake than Wynton. He was a disbarred lawyer! It was only a matter of time before the inevitable moment when she and Magdalena would be invited to their hotel rooms. The idea filled her with dread. She hadn't had a dalliance in months and months and was in some small way grateful for this encounter. Still, she knew if push came to shove, she would feign outrage and refuse any advances.

But the whole thing would be embarrassing.

When her New York strip arrived, Magdalena's ardor for footsie dimmed immediately. She pulled both her feet back and tucked them under her chair and then tucked into the food. While the elders at the table continued to banter, Magdalena lost herself in the ecstasy of Grade-A red meat.

"I was starving, yo!" she said, after obliterating her meal.

"I like a woman with a healthy appetite," mooned Wynton, winking at her, his foot groping the floor in vain.

"You just like women, period," said Davis, laughing.

"You mean he's not very discriminating?" asked Lady Vanessa.

"Oh, I'm very discriminating," Wynton said.

"Really?" said Magdalena, throwing him a scowl. "Discriminating?"

"Very."

"*Discriminating?!*"

"Absolutely!"

"Well, I don't play that racist shit! Damn, Lady Vee! I can't believe I'm playing footsie with a discriminator! My dad is, like, black, yo! He's *biracial!*"

"Footsie?" Lady Vanessa was horrified.

"Racist?" Wynton was confused.

"Let's get out of here!" Magdalena rose from her seat.

"But Maggie, you misunderstand—"

"Nah, nah. Thank you for the steak, but you got the wrong girl, Mr. Discriminator!"

"I'm not—"

"Is all old, rich white men racists, Lady Vee? Or just these fast food men?"

Lady Vanessa was up from her chair as well. She threw the men a look of embarrassment. "Let me see if I can talk her down."

She grabbed her jacket and went after her lady-in-waiting.

She was thrilled. Magdalena's misplaced outrage had saved them both.

"Discriminators, Lady Vee! Can you believe it!"

Lady Vanessa didn't have the heart to deliver a lecture on the nuances of vocabulary and meanings. "Magdalena, don't you even think about those terrible examples of men," she said, turning to the street and throwing up her hand. "Taxi!"

They got into the back seat of the cab, and Lady Vanessa offered a motherly pat on the younger woman's thigh.

"Are you okay, Magdalena? I'm sorry about that."

"Sorry? For that steak? And those grandpas trying to get lucky? Damn! It was all fun."

"Until the end."

"Nah. I just made that shit up. I know he wasn't no racist. I just didn't want no scene with those wrinkly-ass men."

Lady Vanessa was stunned. She clapped her hands. "Oh, Magdalena! That was wonderful."

"You book smart, Lady Vee. I'm street smart."

"You certainly were today."

"I should have waited until after dessert, yo! But when discrimination came up, I had to cash that in."

"Bravo. I'm glad you did. I'm exhausted."

"Me too."

"You can sleep in the guest room. We have had quite a day."

"Hell, yeah, Lady Vee! Portals, cops, artists, millionaires. My crew ain't gonna believe this!"

CHAPTER 10

In which Lady Vanessa attends a costume party, learns the shocking truth about Nelson Dodge, and finds her passion piqued

Lady Vanessa had lived in her large apartment building on the Upper West Side of Manhattan for almost twenty years. The residents of the building loved communal activities and had established a number of annual traditions.

There was a planting weekend every April for the urban gardeners of the building, who would spruce up the small, sunless concrete-based "garden" at the rear of the building. There was the reading library in the basement—a bookcase of constantly shifting titles and Post-it notes with recommended books and wish lists that had inspired the formation of several reading groups. There was a winter coat drive that ran from November until January first.

But the crowning event in the building was the annual Halloween party.

Although most of the units on Lady Vanessa's floor were one- or two-bedroom co-op units carved from the building's original sprawling six- and seven-room spreads, the building still had plenty of apartments with the original layouts intact. This meant there was a robust local population of families with one, two, and even four children and an equally robust population of mothers and nannies who had nothing better to do than devote hours and hours to ensuring the annual Halloween party would be the building's most extravagant event.

Posters adorned the elevators announcing a costume contest for all ages, a lobby parade, a bobbing-for-apples contest with individualized buckets for contestants so that no germs would be spread, Simon Says and Freeze Dancing competitions, and "guest stars," hired entertainers who dressed in Batman, Elmo, and Dora costumes. Pizza would be served, along with popcorn, soft drinks, and goodie bags filled with candy. All in the building's sizable lobby from 5 p.m. to 7 p.m.

A sign-up list to help with the party went up in the building's mailroom. Lady Vanessa, who remembered the days when Emma was in middle school and brought a posse of candy-mad pals to the festivities, had mixed feelings about the screech-filled, high-glucose event. But when she observed that a few women from her floor had signed up, she was not to be outdone and added her name to the list.

Lady Vanessa arrived at the lobby at 4 p.m. on Halloween Day to find chaos in full effect. The Co-op Board President, Madeline Zwik, was asking about the sound system. The super, Rafael, was bringing up folding tables from the basement. Jessica Kessler, the entertainment committee chair, stood on a ladder stringing colorful ribbons along the walls and taping cut-outs of ghosts and ghouls below the streamers.

Lady Vanessa volunteered at the face-painting table. This was a no-brainer assignment for Her Ladyship, who was a makeup fanatic and had taught kindergarten for nearly two decades. Her mission was to paint leopard spots and goofy clown visages on any revelers who asked.

Joining her was Natalie Ringer, her spunky neighbor on the twelfth floor, who was sporting a fetching blonde bob. At first, as they sat at the table waiting for kiddie customers, there was an uneasy silence between them, an aura of discomfort rooted in the embarrassing day Lady Vanessa had slapped the man from Grey's Plumbing in the face. It was also the day Natalie had helped Emma throw out her precious romance books.

"How have you been?" said Natalie after getting a styrofoam cup of coffee from the refreshment table.

"Fine, fine! Never better."

"Oh, good! I'm so glad."

"Yes, I had some troubles a few months back. Being a lady can be very trying these days."

"Yes," said Natalie, assuming her neighbor was referring to women's empowerment issues. "Absolutely."

"I'm glad you agree. My daughter says I'm talking nonsense."

"Well…"

"She's living with a wealthy young man. But he makes no commitments to her! It's an outrage."

"I suppose she has her freedom?"

"Freedom? Does she have a lease in her name? Or his heart in her hand? I think not."

Natalie wasn't sure what to say. She took a sip of coffee. "Well, they are a little young."

"How is your love life?" Lady Vanessa inquired.

Natalie sputtered, spraying coffee on the table. "Oh, I'm so sorry. Your question surprised me."

"No worries," said Lady Vanessa, blotting the mess on the table with a sheet of paper towel. "And forgive me for prying. It's just...you are young and pretty in a city filled with men."

"Well, I'm a waitress. My dating options seem to be limited at the moment to waiters, bartenders, and chefs."

"Ah, I understand."

"You do?"

"Certainly. A queen shall not dally with a footman!"

"Ah," Natalie said, pretending she understood.

"Although sometimes the footman is not, in truth, a footman. Remember *The Duchess's Dilemma* by Amanda Linensilk, an underappreciated Regency classic. There, Duchess Regan's footman truly was a prince, a bastard fathered and ignored by the king. Thank goodness he was able to retrieve the lost signet ring the king once gave his mother during their brief intimacy."

"I must have missed that book."

"I would loan it to you, but my daughter committed the unforgivable crime of throwing it away," Lady Vanessa said, opting not to mention that Natalie had helped obliterate her library. Instead, she added, "But my larger point is, a waiter may not be just a waiter and a chef may not just be a chef."

"Actually, most chefs are pretty much chefs; obsessive-compulsive maniacs who are happy doing the same thing over and over. But you have a point about waiters. A lot of them want to be doing something else, like acting or singing."

"What about men in this building?"

"What about them?"

A mother approached with her daughter, a first-grader wearing a soccer uniform.

"This is my daughter, Harmony," said the mother, who, despite her just-home-from-work pantsuit, had donned a tiara to get in the spirit of things.

"What a fabulous name!" gushed Lady Vanessa. "Would you like your face painted?"

The little girl nodded.

"My name is Lady Vanessa, and this is Natalie. I'm good at drawing leopard spots, and she's an expert at tiger stripes. Which would you like?"

"Tiger stripes," the girl said.

The mother departed, and Harmony sat beside Natalie, who started drawing orange lines on the girl's face.

"Well, it seems to me there are some eligible men who live here," said Lady Vanessa, resuming her line of inquiry. "And surely, with your lovely haircut, you have enticed many of them."

"Thank you. I'm glad you like it," said Natalie. "I haven't seen any men that interest me here. Plus, that can be pretty awkward if it doesn't work out—living in the same building and all."

Lady Vanessa nodded. "You are wise beyond your years."

"I'm thirty-one. So I've got nothing on Harmony here. How old are you? Twelve, right?"

"I'm four and a half!" squeaked the little girl.

"I have been waiting for a gentleman of the building to call on me," said Lady Vanessa, ignoring little Harmony. "But he seems rather oblivious. Sometimes he's all charm and fun. Then it's like I don't even exist."

"That sounds vaguely familiar. Harmony, let me know if I'm hurting you."

"I'm okay."

"Oh, it is *very* common. So many of the greatest love stories in history involve a man who has been blinded by personal trials and can't see the perfect mate before him. In Diana Kite-Davies's *Between a Rock and a Workplace*, Wanda Lustbader does everything imaginable to connect with Roland Dash, the son of her boss."

"Right! I remember that. She brings him cookies at work, volunteers to help him on make-or-break deals, stakes out his neighborhood, joins the same gym. And then she finally gets drunk at the office Christmas party and practically throws herself at him."

"Exactly. But she had no way of knowing he was wracked with grief over the tragic fatal illness of his beloved twin sister and is terrified the same disease will strike him. And Wanda also has no idea the weight of the entire company is on his shoulders, no thanks to his father's gambling habits and the blackmail attempts of a former lover, and that Roland is trying to resolve those matters in secret."

"What are you guys talking about?" Harmony asked.

"Boring grown-up stuff," said Natalie. "Say, Harmony, would you like a red nose for fun?"

"Oh, yes, please."

"Okay. We'll do that in a sec.… It is a great book. But that situation is pretty rare, don't you think?"

"Who knows what secrets plague the paramours of our destiny?" said Lady Vanessa gravely.

Natalie was putting the finishing touches on Harmony when Lady Vanessa spotted Nelson Dodge getting out of the elevator.

"Here he is now!" her Ladyship chirped.

"Who? Nelson?"

"Yes. Isn't he handsome?"

Natalie opened her mouth and then closed it again.

"Vanessa! Natalie! Oh, my goodness, who is this adorable soccer-playing tiger?"

"I'm Harmony!"

"Give us a roar, Harmony."

"Raaarrrrrr!"

"Raarrrrrrr!" Nelson laughed as she ran off. "I love Halloween. It really should be a national holiday. You must love it, too, Vanessa. Your time-travel outfits are perfect for it!"

Lady Vanessa turned a deep shade of crimson. "I beg your pardon?"

"I love Vanessa's gowns. I think they're absolutely daring and gorgeous," said Natalie.

"I'm just kidding, Lady Vee. I love that your friend Magdalena calls you that."

"My accoutrements are in keeping with those of a lady. I don't know what else you would expect me to wear."

"What's your costume, Nelson?" said Natalie.

"I'm getting changed at a friend's house in the Village. We're going as the Supremes. I'm going to be Diana Ross, of course!"

"Fantastic. I hope you take some pictures."

"Will do. Gotta run. Bye!"

"Bye," said Natalie.

The two women sat in silence for a brief moment.

"How dare he!"

"Vanessa," said Natalie.

"Mocking my sense of style!"

"Yes, that wasn't very nice. He's a little…"

"Self-centered?"

"Yes, that too."

"And foolish. Diana Ross! He should be a knight. Like Lancelot or Galahad."

"Lady Vanessa, do you remember those books you had on your shelf? I think one was called *Rawhide Mountain*?"

"Of course, by Mickey Gallant? That was so moving when Roy and Chuck finally realized they shared the same secret."

"Well, I get the sense that maybe…"

"Yes?"

"Maybe Nelson Dodge has more in common with those characters than you realize."

"Nelson? You mean…? But I often see him with women. This very tall blonde named Jezebel. And a rather rotund woman named Starlight."

"I think those are stage names. Jezebel's hair isn't really blonde, either. And I'm pretty sure it's not her own hair."

"You are trying to tell me that Nelson's friends…"

"Are into drag."

"But he's not into drag. What are you suggesting?"

"I'm trying to tell you that Nelson isn't going to be interested in you or me or Scarlett Johansson, for that matter. Romantically speaking."

Lady Vanessa was silent. Natalie looked away.

"I am so embarrassed," Lady Vanessa said.

"Don't be. You wouldn't be the first to have your gaydar distorted by a crush."

Tears were pooling in Lady Vanessa's eyes. She felt utterly humiliated. She looked down at the face paint kit in front of her. "Oh my, I don't have enough orange," she said, standing up. "I need to go upstairs for a moment."

"Take your time."

"I'll be right back," she said, her voice cracking.

TRANSLATOR'S NOTE #5

As you are about to see, once again, the mysterious Aisha Cide Benengeli has interrupted her manuscript. Or is it truly an interruption? Perhaps you will begin to see it, as I have, as a calculation. An addition to the story. A part of the novel. This time she provides more personal details. So many that I have endeavored to find out who, exactly, this jaw-droppingly talented author is. Many Egyptian diplomats raised daughters in America. But there is no organization that tracks this particular group of ex-patriots. I have reached out to the current and former information officers at the Egyptian Embassy, but they have been no help. In fact, they further clouded the issue by noting there are embassy diplomats and United Nations diplomats and covert diplomats—spies!—who work undercover for nongovernmental organizations like the World Bank or embedded in multinational companies. Tracking Benengeli, which, as I will now recount, I had at first assumed was her married name, is impossible without knowing her father's name.

But that assumption was completely wrong. I am now 99.99999 percent certain Benengeli is a pseudonym. Consider the following facts: In Chapter Seven, when Benengeli first introduces herself, she worries that she will be dismissed when she is compared to, in her words, "the unmatchable genius of Miguel de Cervantes and his Adventures of Don Quixote.*" Thinking about her anxiety, I pulled my copy of* Quixote *off the shelf. While rereading the book, I was confronted with a forgotten and telling detail: Benengeli is the name Cervantes gives as the "true" author of* Don Quixote*! It becomes clear that the* *name of the author of* Lady Vanessa of Manhattanshire—*Aisha Benengeli—is a ruse, a joke, a cipher, a dodge, a puzzle, a shout-out to Cervantes, and yes, utterly infuriating, for how will we ever discover the beautiful mind behind this tale? And how will we know if the author's own story, which grows more complex and painful, is true? Or is it, too, a ruse? A false flag? A ploy to win our sympathy? For all we truly know, this entire book could be an elaborately staged hoax written by a professor at a community college in Des Moines or a hack tabloid writer in Los Angeles!*

Given that the original manuscript was written in Arabic, however, and that it was found in a designer handbag and that I have been to the Four Seasons hotel in Alexandria and it is indeed heavenly, I believe the story of Aisha Benengeli, or whatever her real name is, that follows is true. I will explain why at a later point.

CHAPTER 11

In which the author confesses her despair over love

And so, we are now two-thirds of the way through Lady Vanessa's trials. And as the Greek playwrights dictated, according to my professor at the small liberal arts college where I lost my virginity to a boy named Joshua Oscar Wertz, at the end of the second act, the heroine is as far away from her goal as can be. And indeed, Lady Vanessa is heartbroken, filled with doubt, and questioning her fundamental beliefs and her future. Like all heroines at this point, she is engulfed by despair, her mind swirling with thoughts of collapse, of quitting, of spinsterhood, and even of suicide.

I know these thoughts too well. Even as I write from what some might consider a modern-day paradise—my luxurious four-room suite overlooking the beach and ocean waters of Alexandria—I, too, despair. Although the casual observer might think my every whim and wish is being catered to by an attentive staff, the thing I covet the most—enduring torrid, carnal abandon with my heart's true love—is not within reach.

My husband... What is there to say? I can barely bring myself to touch him. Two years ago, my illusion, or rather, my illusion of his illusion, exploded when his name surfaced in news reports.

He was not, as I had been led to believe, merely a very successful man involved in import and export, the owner of an international shipping firm, Dikahn Delivery. He was the billionaire who engineered enormous kickbacks for officials who bought weapons and supplies from Weaptron Industries, Satilicon and Militagistics, all companies he owned or co-owned. I had had no clue.

I know it is difficult to believe that I, a reasonably intelligent, multilingual, well-traveled woman who once worked for a humanitarian international aid organization, did not know my own husband made his considerable fortune—*our* considerable fortune—selling weapons of destruction.

"You must have been in denial," my old roommate Annabella told me when the headlines in the *Guardian* first splashed his secret.

But that wasn't the case. I had asked my husband about his work many times. In addition to his shipping company, he had "investments" and "real estate deals all over the world." That is why he would travel. That is why, he would tell me, he met with heads of state.

Sometimes I accompanied him. While he had meetings in Kampala or Johannesburg or Manila, I would work on my writing, meet with women in the diplomatic corps, or go to the spa.

Perhaps I should have wondered why, at elaborate state dinners, there were so many military officers at the table.

Perhaps I knew that the lack of details my husband shared with me—"Just shipping and logistics, darling, the boring nuts and bolts of modern life"—allowed us to save face with each other. Or for him to save face with me.

But it was bombs and bullets, not nuts and bolts, that my elegant husband was focusing on. And the hardware needed to launch them: automatic machine guns, rocket launchers, jets, helicopters, and drones. Of course, Dikahn Delivery handled all the shipping.

I read a second report in the *Times*. He was Assad's biggest provider. I thought of the images I had seen of Aleppo in Syria, the ancient, bomb-ravaged, decaying skeleton of a city that looked worse than Dresden.

I was angry. Devastated. I thought I had married a businessman. Just another member of the privileged class who knew how to use money to make more money, like the fathers—sorry, ladies, they were always fathers, never mothers—of my classmates at the small liberal arts college I attended.

These men were invariably in "finance" or "real estate." Or were presidents or vice presidents of corporations or banks. I had always assumed they made their money by running their businesses well. Or by investing or inheriting well. Or by playing the financial instruments of Wall Street with the skill of maestros. I thought my husband was like these other men—that he shared their skills. He could buy low and sell high. Actually, in his case, the modus operandi was often buy high first, then pay off the corrupt military or government official authorized to do deals and sell much, much higher.

I told him I needed space. He said he understood. "We are both victims of circumstance," he said.

"I'm not sure that's an accurate assessment," I said. "Right now, I feel like I'm a victim of *your* circumstances."

"I suppose." He looked around the immaculate mansion we owned, casting his eyes over paintings by Seurat and Miró and the mid-century furniture from Denmark. "Pretty opulent circumstances, though."

I left our home in Kensington—London, not Brooklyn—and went to Egypt. To my parents' home.

"What is so wrong?" my mother asked later.

"Is that a serious question?"

"Of course."

"He lied to me."

"He lied to protect you."

"He lied to have me. To win me. I wouldn't have had a cup of coffee with him, never mind married him, if I'd known how he really made his money."

"He sells a service. Many services."

"Services! Tell that to the dead of Aleppo. He went to Damascus at least *four* times last year. I thought he was in Jordan."

"There will always be someone out there doing what he does."

"What he does is a choice. When I met him, he told me he had enough money to never work again. And yet..."

"Work can be addictive. Look at your father. He would still go to the office every day. Thank Allah for mandatory retirement."

"Did you know? Did Daddy know?"

"What does it matter?"

I took that as an affirmative. My parents certainly knew. Or knew something.

I left my parents' house and moved to the hotel. The suite.

I used the credit cards he had given me to pay for everything.

He wrote me emails.

I wrote: "*Aleppo? Really?*"

He wrote back: "Those were surveillance equipment deals. Night vision goggles…jeep tires."

I didn't believe him.

I took one of my credit cards and went to a well-known jewelry store and bought $200,000 worth of diamonds. I went to Cairo and sold the jewels for $165,000. I sent the money to the Syrian Relief Fund and the International Rescue Fund. I did that every few weeks or so, buying gold necklaces, rubies, sapphires. Sometimes I kept the money for myself.

We didn't talk for months. Finally, my husband asked about my "buying spree." I told him what I was doing. He sighed. He didn't ask me to stop, though.

He also called me when he received a bill from the divorce lawyer I had consulted.

"You're divorcing me?"

"I don't know."

Silence.

"On what grounds would you divorce me?"

I thought about saying, consorting with war criminals. But I said, "Deception."

He laughed his elegant laugh. The one that I remember once thinking was so warm and understanding. He said, "Who deceived whom, darling?"

"I never lied to you."

"I never said you did."

He hung up. I puzzled over his question. If he wasn't accusing me of lying and he wasn't admitting that he had lied to me, then what was he saying?

He could only mean that I had deceived myself.

Did I?

Does it matter if I did?

I sought refuge in my suite and began to scrape together the story of Lady Vanessa. Did I start this story because I felt fooled by love? Yes. Because I was angry at love? Yes. Because I had settled and not followed my heart? Yes.

But also, I wrote because it was an escape for me. Just as reading is a wonderful distraction, so is writing. And when the going gets tough, it is, for me, the better distraction. Or the more distracting distraction.

I wanted to mock love, to roast the quest, and yet somehow leave readers with a sense of hope, the same hope I wanted for myself.

You're probably wondering, *What hope does Lady Vanessa impart? Is she more than a punchline punching bag?*

All I can say is, wait.

I had a husband who was what so many romance books would describe as an alpha male. Yes, he was on the shorter side of hunkdom. But he was fit and trim. And rich. A billionaire. He pursues the things in life he wants. He buys them.

Me? Was I bought? If you had asked me before, I would have said no. But I see now that I allowed myself to embrace the idea that this wealthy man was desirable, partly because he was wealthy, and that he would satisfy my parents and satisfy me. He was, I thought, as good as it would get for me.

I'm sure all these theories feed into the book before you. I wrote and rewrote in a fever. For three months I ordered room service, sat on my balcony, and rarely left the suite. There were days when the only person I saw or talked to was Fatima, the maid who cleaned my rooms. She was young and very hardworking. She scrubbed bathroom tiles in a fury, getting down on her hands and knees each day and attacking them. Once, I tried to get her to ease up.

"It's still clean from yesterday, Fatima. Just wipe it down."

"I must. Hotel standards. I could be fired, madame."

"I could tell them I ordered you not to clean my bathroom."

She smiled and continued her assault on the tile.

I ordered room service: tea for two with almond pastries and cucumber sandwiches. When Fatima was done cleaning, I asked her to eat with me. "Just once. Sit for five minutes, rest, and have tea, and then you can go."

We sat together, sipping and noshing in silence. She finished a sandwich and a pastry. And then she said, "Thank you, madame. I've never had such fine food."

"Well, thank you, Fatima. It's nice to see you sitting for once!"

She hopped to her feet. "I must be going."

Me and my big mouth.

I think she appreciated my comment and my lame attempt at basic kindness, however, because a few weeks later she came to see me when I was lounging on the balcony. Broom in hand, she addressed me directly, something she had never done before.

"Madame," she said. "There are men asking about you."

"Me?"

"Yes. I was offered five hundred dollars to talk. US dollars."

"Talk about what? Me?"

"To tell them about you. There were two men. They ask what you do. Who else comes here? Are there any male visitors?"

"Really?"

"I told them we are not allowed to discuss our guests. Hotel policy. But they kept asking questions."

"Oh dear. I hope they didn't bully you."

"No, I walked on."

"I am very grateful. Maybe I should give you five hundred dollars."

"That is not necessary, madame. I was following hotel policy."

I assumed my husband had sent these men.

I wondered about the timing. Only recently, hit by a bout of writer's block, had I slowed down on my writing. In addition to the short book you are reading, I had been working on another, less funny and more dramatic novel, as well as short stories and poems. But the "serious" novel was wearing on me. I shifted my focus to *Lady Vanessa*.

I was burning out. I realized that I had been alone now, grieving in my way, for more than two years. I had only been married for ten! What was I doing? Who was I hiding from? What was I waiting for?

I had been deceiving myself. My husband was right. I had been deceiving myself for decades!

Ever since I left for college.

That was when the deception was writ large. When the chorus of mind control began. From the moment I stepped into the orientation session at my small liberal arts college and looked at all those boys and felt paralyzed, transfixed, and beguiled, wracked with anxiety about whether any of them would find me attractive, I countered my nerves with a mantra instilled by my mother: *fully compatible, fully compatible, fully compatible.*

Yes, these were the only two words that mattered.

How many of these blossoming young men at my school were "fully compatible?" How many even thought for one second about such a thing? Not one!

Few, if any, suffered the eternal crisis of old-world parental approval. I had already been indoctrinated for years. The threats! My mother's tears. The misguided, fabricated horror stories fueled by the hate, distrust, paranoia, and ignorance that comes with tribalism. How Christians hush up thousands of baptismal drownings every year! How Jews control the world and bury their dead with blank checks to buy their way into heaven! How Shiites plan to annihilate Sunni men and take their women! This is the kind of paranoid madness I was subjected to during every visit home from college.

Who would imagine that my own mother, a well-traveled, cultured woman who had been educated by French Sisters in Alexandria, spouted such paranoid drivel? My mother once sat on the PTA and shared coffee with Miriam Schwartz, the perpetually broke and struggling divorced mom of my best friend

Sara in fifth grade, a Jew who couldn't pay for school lunch, never mind control the world. She should have known better!

At the start of every college semester, I was cautioned about my maidenhood. About white Lotharios, about Black Mandingos, about Hispanic Don Juans and diabolical Asian Fu Manchus, as if my school was populated by a veritable United Nations of stereotypical predatory men.

Men who were the opposite of "fully compatible."

Of course, I did have boyfriends and sex. Most of those boys were loves of the present, not the future. But there was one who, finally, I adored, one who made me feel so loved and loving that it hurt. His name, appropriately enough, was Grant Hart, a name straight out of a romance novel.

He was a year older than me. He studied environmental science, but we met in a studio art class. He asked if he could draw me. Soon we were inseparable. He would walk me to classes and then wait for the class to end so he could walk with me again. I was in awe of him, his size, his strength, his perfectly aligned face, his idealism, his kindness. I thought of him all the time. But periodically, whenever I felt myself growing too enamored, too happy, I would remind Grant—and myself—that we were not fully compatible and therefore had no future together. He was born a nonbeliever, an infidel, and even though I was, too, he would never be good enough for my parents.

He said he understood. How I wish that he said he didn't! How I wish he had fought me, fought *for* me! But perhaps I sold my story of our differences too well. Perhaps, for Grant, joining the Peace Corps to teach water management in an impoverished village in Niger seemed easier than dealing with me and my family, seemed less painful than fighting a battle I told him he'd lose. He should have never listened to me. But he did. And he left for West Africa.

As I got older, my mother worried that I would become an old maid. My twice-a-year visits home to their big house in Alexandria were spiked with frequent dinner parties, always with single men at the table.

Single men who did not hold a candle to Grant Hart.

Until, finally, almost two decades after leaving school, I met my husband under the watchful shadow of my parents. He was urbane, older, with perfect manners, perfect hair, and perfect shoes that looked like they might walk by themselves. He was charming. His name was Ayman, and he looked vaguely like Omar Sharif but without the over-the-top macho sheen.

I had to allow for the seventeen years between us. I had to allow that he studied backgammon and cricket like mullahs study the Koran. He was an Egyptian by way of London and Paris and Wall Street. He invited me to visit him in London. We went gallery hopping. He took me to the British Museum to see the Rosetta Stone, which he considered Egypt's greatest creation: "the document that shows our nation its brilliant past."

I liked him. Did I love him? I told myself that I could. Now I think I just loved that this desirable man desired me. I married him.

I never expected to find that this polite, charming, import-export billionaire was a liar and agent of destruction, a more palatable term for what he truly was: a merchant of death.

Actually, that's not true. I know that all men lie sometimes, just as women sometimes do. I just thought that, with me, it would be different.

But truly, I never expected to find that my husband was a killer-by-proxy...a war profiteer.

Is there anything more wretched?

It was the most important discovery of my life.

Until I opened my email and saw the name Grant Hart.

To say I read the email he sent would be an understatement. I devoured it. I examined it over and over, reading each word. I printed it out and inhaled the paper, imagining the generic ink was imbued with his scent.

He wrote to say that he had obtained my email address from an old classmate and that he hoped I didn't mind. He wanted to tell me something that he felt was important, but he didn't want to intrude on my life. (See? Even Grant Hart lies. Of course, he wanted to intrude. How do I know that? By writing, he was intruding.) He wrote to say that he had thought of me every day for twenty-five years.

I wrote back and confessed the exact same thing.

I've started to think about something that should be news to no one: that love can be fatal.

Every day, I log on to websites to read the news, and I am swarmed with reports of gun deaths in America. The mass murders! The drug murders! These are horrible. But there are suicides, too, thousands and thousands each year, and at their center, sure, there is depression, mental illness, and debt. But I'm convinced many are love—or lack of love—related. Then add the domestic murders! I'm sure I will be pilloried for this, but how many of these murders are what the world once called crimes of passion, in which love, or some crazed, horrible, lethal mutant form of it, morphs into anger, hatred, and rage and then kills?

Now love kills me. I struggle with Lady Vanessa. To find a way for her, somehow, to beat the insurmountable odds against her. To rescue her, not only from herself and her madness but the madness of life. I mean, think of it! A woman nearly fifty! In gay-friendly New York, where single, straight men of commensurate age may be in want of a wife but are likely damaged beyond all hope of cohabitation, either physically, emotionally, or financially. What are the odds I can marry her off (such a terrible phrase for a woman I've come to adore) in a manner that won't defy credibility? How can I transform her?

Just as urgently, will I have time to do it?

TRANSLATOR'S NOTE #6

Dear readers, as you know, I have struggled to determine the true identity of our mysterious author, Aisha Benengeli, from the moment of my first encounter with Lady Vanessa. Based on the information in the preceding chapter, I believe I have the answer. But given the nature of the work and the levels of delusion and deception on display, I remain slightly guarded, concerned that perhaps this is a form of misdirection. Could this be the work of a deceitful author looking to plant a false attribution of this bewitching book on an unsuspecting reader? Perhaps. But in my heart of hearts, I don't think that's the case. Aisha Benengeli has clearly poured her passion and knowledge into Lady Vanessa. And the discursions into her personal life—her insights into the struggle to write, her feelings for Lady Vanessa, and now, her unfettered, naked, deeply private disclosures—have me convinced the biographical details are the stuff of fact, not fiction.

Indeed, a simple internet search on the terms "Egyptian arms dealer wife" returns the name Rana Abboud, the wife of Ayman Abboud, the veiled owner of Militagistics, which bills itself as "A Global Defense and Strategy Solutions Company," and Dikahn Delivery.

A search on Rana Abboud leads to several links to literary magazines where she published short fiction. One site contains the following author bio:

> "Rana Abboud was born in Alexandria, Egypt, and raised in America. She is grateful for both events. She works for a nonprofit agency and dreams of writing full time."

Accompanying these three sentences is a headshot of the author. Her smile is wide and full, made bigger by the pixie cut that frames her small, delicate face. There is a hint of crow's feet at the edge of her right eye, but other than that she looks utterly fresh faced; it's impossible to tell if she's twenty-three or thirty-three. She looks like a darker-hued Audrey Hepburn.

Further searches reveal Rana attended Hampden College in Vermont. Sources at the Egyptian Consulate in New York identified Rana's father as Rahim Hamdy. A search on his name turned up a shock: Rahim and his wife Shani were victims of a home invasion in 2017 in Alexandria. And just a few months later, the couple vanished into thin air. The news article reported their daughter, Rana, "the reclusive author wife of billionaire Ayman Abboud, has not been seen in recent months."

Now that I have discovered the true identity of the creator of Lady Vanessa, I feel strangely out of sorts. I want more information about her, but recent news on Rana Abboud is nonexistent. There are countless photos of her and Ayman out and about at charity dinners and cricket matches. But then, also around 2017, she vanishes.

CHAPTER 12

In which Lady Vanessa and Mr. Miller find common ground

It took Lady Vanessa a mere twenty minutes to recover from the realization that the object of her affection, Nelson Dodge, was gay. What had it cost her, really? Nothing other than mental and emotional energy. Ten or maybe forty frivolous rides on the vertical chariot, hoping to catch him going out with his poodle for a walk. A few faux giggles at his jokes. Wasted interest in his acting and voice-over career. A few hours or days transported into a fantasy involving the total devotion of his manly charms to her pleasure. That was it.

Except....

What would Magdalena say? Of all the fallout from her misguided infatuation, this loomed as the most damaging. What would happen when she told Magdalena? Or what if the young woman already knew! What if the same traits that tipped off Natalie registered with Magdalena too?

She would never hear the end of it. Magdalena would think she was a sham, nothing but an old fool! Just like the duped spinsters who lurked in the shadows of so many books, another cautionary tale, a victim, the collateral damage of a world where so many women are taken advantage of and then discarded or simply—and perhaps worse—forgotten and ignored. Was there any crueler reality than being stripped of dignity and rendered invisible?

She paced back and forth in her apartment, searching for a tactic. Surely, one of her books must have dealt with this scenario. Estelle Nova? Lady Catherine Cunnington? Monique de la Croix? Hope Hendrix? Sophia Fall-Bellows? Lady Vanessa reviewed dozens of her favorite authors and their brilliant novels, but nothing came to mind.

She would have to think of something herself. A story that would absolve her. And then, out of nowhere, a line popped into her head—from a song, not a book! And she could practically see Nelson Dodge singing the lyric while decked out in his Diana Ross costume!

"I'm coming out!" Lady Vanessa sang, copying Diana as best she could, which meant warbling in a constantly shifting key.

She would tell Magdalena how Nelson cornered her at the Halloween party and made a tearful, shocking confession to her about recently discovering his true nature. And how he couldn't hide it anymore. How he didn't want to lead any more women on and how, most importantly, he didn't want to lead himself on. It was time, she imagined him saying, smiling through his tears, to face up to the truth.

Yes! This was the scenario she would present to Magdalena. And while she was at it, she would turn it into a cautionary tale of love's illusory dangers, and why pedigree, reputation, and class, none of which she had truly known about Nelson Dodge, are so often essential when determining a worthy mate.

She grabbed some orange blush and returned to the building lobby.

The Halloween party was filling up with Dora the Explorers, Spider-Mans, ballerinas, princesses, Harry Potters, robots, vampires, and other costumed kids. But business at the face-painting table was slow for Lady Vanessa and Natalie. And when Mr. Miller, that older fellow inhabitant of the twelfth floor, stepped out of the elevator wearing his always-present tweed blazer and lugging a portable easel, the two women watched him survey the chaos and then waved as he looked in their direction.

"Is he gay too?" asked Lady Vanessa.

"I doubt it. My gaydar is flatlining."

"I am so embarrassed. I consider myself an expert in all aspects of love and romance. Please, keep this to yourself."

"Of course!"

"Hello, ladies," said Mr. Miller. "Happy Halloween!"

"Boo!" said Natalie. "Are you going out to work?"

"I thought I'd draw some of the kids. If they'll pose long enough."

"Good luck with that. Sugar, pizza, soda, and costumes. They'll be as hopped up as meth heads. Or the coked-up chefs at my restaurant."

"I'm sure a princess or ballerina will sit for you," said Lady Vanessa. "My daughter would have been thrilled to have her portrait painted."

"I'm not exactly a painter. I'm more of an illustrator. A cartoonist and caricature artist."

"Did you study somewhere?"

"No. I'm self-taught. I'm a face man. I can draw anything, anime saucer eyes, exploding old-man eyebrows, super jowls, apple cheeks, or modelized high cheekbones."

"What is your favorite feature to draw?"

"Noses are my thing."

"Oh, dear. Really?"

"Noses and hair are the closest thing humans have to horns, the closest thing we have to saying, 'Hey! Look at me!' The nose sits there in the middle of everyone's face, impossible to miss. It comes in all shapes and sizes. Mega honkers, tiny buttons, upturned like the chutes for ski jump competitions, super flared, flattened, aquiline, Greco-big, Greco-small, the Asiatic spreader, the Uncle Mortie—a soused schnozzle with an alcohol-infused vermillion patina—the WASP, that patrician elegance, the mosquito, which is narrow and pointy and severe."

"And what are our noses?" asked Natalie.

"Ah, that's easy. You have a button-cute Irish Rose. Vanessa has the Esther, a.k.a. the Winehouse."

"The Esther?"

"The Jewish Queen. Who can resist? It's long, it's narrow. It's dynamite!"

"The Esther!" This time Lady Vanessa laughed.

"If you want to get technical, it's just a few degrees removed from the Cleopatra and a distant cousin of the Helen of Troy."

"Where do you get these names?" asked Natalie.

"I'm a scholar. I have my own taxonomy. From years of cartooning and probing the proboscis, as it were. You know, in my job you have to have fun. You're messing with people's vanity, which is serious, serious stuff. It's good to have a spiel. Tell you what, let me set up my easel, and let's see if we can't get some clients."

In the space of five minutes, Mr. Miller unfolded his rig, knocked out a hilarious self-portrait, and created a sign: *Free Cartoons by World Famous Artist!*

"I'm nothing if not modest." He winked at Lady Vanessa and Natalie.

When a third-grade ballerina stopped by, he instructed her to have her face painted first. "And then I'll draw you."

And thus began a production line, first of the building's princesses, Doc McStuffins, Ariels, and Doras, but then, as the mothers began to see the results of Mr. Miller's hilarious, spot-on portraits, the boys in attendance were summoned to sit as well. The artisans of the twelfth floor made a happy trio. Mr. Miller's benevolence, of course, had an ulterior motive: to make the well-heeled populace of the building aware of his artistry.

He had no doubt commissions would roll in, thanks to the vanishing stack of business cards he had placed on his easel. But he also felt a spark of interest from the younger Lady Vanessa and, to a lesser degree, from the much younger Natalie Ringer.

He was, of course, deluded about the thirty-years-younger Natalie. She was feeling upbeat, but that had more to do with the entire Halloween vibe at the makeup table. Working nights in a restaurant was, she was sure, bad for the soul. She had long suspected that working with kids—making art with them—was a much more gratifying experience. And this was proving to be true. Plus, she was relieved to see that Lady Vanessa's shattered composure had been vanquished. Her neighbor was positively beaming in the presence of Mr. Miller. It was as if Nelson Dodge had never existed.

Indeed, Natalie Ringer's observation, if anything, under-estimated Lady Vanessa's state of mind. As she powder-puffed, bespotted, and glittered her young charges, Her Ladyship's mind was racing, revving in overdrive with thoughts of Mr. Miller, a gentleman who was obviously ten times the man that Nelson Dodge was.

She wondered how to engineer more meetings with this amusing man who lived right next door. At first, she thought of arranging a floor-wide potluck dinner hosted in her apart-ment. But when she did the math, Natalie, Arlene the retired librarian, and Tammy Feathers the never-at-home workaholic Wall Streeter represented three potential rivals for Mr. Miller's interest. That would never do. No, she would ask him to din-ner. Was that too forward? Probably. Maybe she would bake a pie and bring it over. Oh, dear. How did this used to work?

She had met her ex-husband, Joseph, at college, when courtship was driven by everyone's youthful looks and dat-ing. Hooking up and having a boyfriend were in the air twenty-four-seven.

The official line of colleges everywhere is that students are there to study, to focus on academics. The well-rounded student was also interested in studying drinking, drug consumption, and sex—or, if not sex, intimate relationships, which led to sex. In Lady Vanessa's case—she was known at the time as Maxine—this had led to Joseph. Or had led Joseph to her. They married two years after graduating.

Dating, though, had not been part of her life for some time. After she and Joseph split and Emma was old enough to go to summer camp, Lady Vanessa would spend July and August attending singles weekends, answering personals, and placing personals. She went on dates. There were a few passing flings, but none of her suitors ignited a true, instant thunderclap of desire.

The few men she deemed acceptable eventually proved to be unacceptable too. But this man, Mr. Miller…he seemed different. Genuine. Handsome in a craggy way. Both his hands and mind darted as he worked, a warm smile engaging his subject. He would kibitz with the kids, intentionally getting the obvious wrong. "Let me get this straight, your eyes are black?" he'd ask a blue-eyed girl. "How long have you been a fan of Batman?" he'd ask a boy dressed as Spider-Man. The kids exploded with laughter at this foolish grownup. No wonder there was a line of costumed kids waiting to be drawn.

As Lady Vanessa watched him, she envisioned dropping off some cookies or inviting him to tea or asking if he had any interest in going to an exhibition at the Metropolitan Museum or—maybe this was a good idea—requesting her own caricature. She didn't want to seem too forward.

A lady must always be a lady after all.

CHAPTER 13

In which a lady pauses for rest and reflection

The next day, Lady Vanessa took to her bed.

When Magdalena arrived and asked what was wrong, she complained of an upset stomach and sent her devoted lady-in-waiting home to Brooklyn. When Emma, alerted by Magdalena, called and asked for further details about her health, Lady Vanessa sighed and gave a more precise diagnosis.

"Men."

"Men?" asked Emma. "What does that mean?"

"It means my heart is heavy. I am betrayed and yet bewitched."

Emma was silent for a moment. "Mom, are you bingeing on those books again?"

"*Those* books? You mean the books that have sustained me? The stories that give me hope that somewhere, sometime there will be a partner who will not abandon me, who will worship me, all of me, my faults, my blemishes, my kindness, my curves and wrinkles, my decorum, and yes, not recoil when he ignites my hot-blooded, unbridled passion? *Those* books? Yes,

I'm currently seeking solace in Gloria Gaston-Glee's mesmerizing *The Poetic Soldier*."

"What's that one about?"

"It is set in the Vietnam War era. The hero, Trent Frisson, rescues a Vietnamese teenager named Thuong and helps her escape to Thailand where she has to work as a bargirl-slash-prostitute until he finds her and takes her away to America."

"A *teenager*?"

"Yes. He sends Thuong beautiful love poems, which allow her to cope with her vile day job at the hands of wicked, violent pimps. And then, when he finally arrives, he slashes their throats to stop them ever abusing women again."

"Mom, you have got to stop reading this garbage. He sounds like a cold-blooded killer and maybe even a sicko-pedophile. I feel creeped out just hearing about that."

"Well, it's different on the page. The poems are lovely."

"Mom, my child support ends from Dad in a few months. What are you going to do when that money dries up?"

"I have some savings. And I have this apartment. Maybe I'll rent out a room."

"Good! Great. I'll throw out all the rest of your books."

"No, you will not."

"Mom, you have an addiction. Those books are like a drug to you. They control your life and dominate your personality."

"Addicted to books?" scoffed Lady Vanessa. "What absolute poppycock!"

"You know, Mom, the church on Amsterdam and 97th has an Al-Anon meeting Monday through Thursday. I'm happy to go with you."

"Balderdash! Stuff and nonsense! These books give me solace. They give me hope. Would you tell a Christian to stop reading the Bible?"

"Actually, yes. Religion is the opiate of the masses."

"Spoken like an arrogant twenty-one-year-old! Who are you to pass judgment?"

"I'm your daughter, and I'm worried about your mental health."

"Thank you for your concern, Emma. But I am quite able to live without these books."

"Prove it!"

"Goodbye, dear."

⸎

That night as she lay in bed, Lady Vanessa began to wonder if her annoying daughter might have a point. Emma was a pain. She called her Maxine or Mom instead of Lady Vanessa. She had decimated a library of sacred texts after the showdown with that awful Christian Grey, a cad who, Lady Vanessa was now ready to concede, might have been a plumber. And her daughter had also thrown out her first hoop skirt. But Emma did seem, on some level, to be motivated by love and concern for her.

Lady Vanessa looked over at her night table where Deliliah del Dulcet's *The Singer and the Saxman* was sitting and reached for it.

She admired the smoky photograph of a swarthy man in a suit with narrow lapels. He was clutching a beautiful brunette woman with a sensuous, ruby-lipped mouth who was whispering in his ear.

Falling in love with an artist must be complicated. They were always traveling, working, showing off, expressing themselves. Mr. Miller was an artist. The few times they had met before Halloween, he seemed quiet and calm. A big, reserved man. Maybe it was the tweed jacket.

That professorial air had evaporated yesterday at the Halloween party. He was witty, warm, charming, and solicitous. He was funny. He seemed kind. Lady Vanessa wondered if it was an act. She put the book back on her night table. She didn't need to read; Emma was making a big deal out of nothing.

She recalled Mr. Miller telling her she had an Esther of a nose. She wondered if he was a nose-rubber. One of the books caught in Emma's purge had been an edition of a chaste Canadian classic, *Eskimo-Kisses*, by Marjorie Stewart. Oh, to read that now! Lady Vanessa shut her eyes, but she was not tired. Mr. Miller was still on her mind. She rolled over and retrieved *The Singer and the Saxman*. She was glad it had escaped Emma's library cleansing. She read for a while and fell asleep around midnight.

CHAPTER 14

In which the author risks everything...for everything

I too have read deep into the night and never more fervently than I have now, hoping to lose myself in Lady Vanessa's story. How strange that reading can inspire madness—never mind Vanessa, just look at all the crazy, paranoid behavior by Americans reading Reddit and Twitter!—and yet reading can save us from madness too.

Two weeks ago, I flew to Paris. I had considered dashing off an email to my husband about how I was meeting three friends from college for a reunion celebrating our semester abroad so many years ago. But that would have been a lie.

He had lied to me, and I wanted to keep the moral high ground.

So I just left.

I told myself he didn't deserve the truth. He could live in darkness when it came to me. He already lived surrounded by darkness, in my opinion. A middleman to slaughter. I'm sure he justified the sale of arms to protect the world order. The status quo. "Armies exist to ensure peace" is the standard operating logic for military men world over, contradictory as it is.

What is my argument? I exist on his largesse. I haven't worked in the ten years since we married. I am still living a life of opulence and privilege funded by the sale of products that kill, maim, and destroy. I benefit from that. Yes, I can try and make amends or gestures of peace, writing huge checks using my maiden name to UNICEF, International Rescue Committee, Doctors Without Borders, and others.

I guess, to some degree, it's my slight, modern-day improvement on the pardons sold during the Middle Ages that allowed donors to buy their way into heaven. My hypocrisy is vile, isn't it? It gets worse. I can't honestly say that bombs and Syria were the ultimate drivers of my flight to Paris. Yes, they helped me justify the trip. But truly, this is what happens when Grant Hart tells you he's flying from Madagascar to Paris.

If the other stuff hadn't happened, would I still have gone? If my husband and I had children? If our fortune was somehow cleaner? I don't know. If all that had happened hadn't happened, would I have gone? I wanted love. I wanted passion. Complacency and convenience are diseases. Everything we do now in our digital devolution is about making life easier, about taking less effort.

Digital delivery, home delivery, crowdsourcing, Uber, the proximity of the cloud...our phones, the new fetishized love object that people can't bear to be away from, that we sleep next to, that we check over and over and over. It is an object that we (and I include myself here) feel we *cannot live without.* And that loaded phrase echoes the exact same feeling of true love, a relationship, a bond that feels more important than life itself.

And yet, how do we find true love now? On an app, via an algorithm that is transmitted to our computers and—irony alert!—our irreplaceable phones?

I could not live without seeing Grant Hart.

That is how I felt.

But to say I was in love? I'm not sure.

What I missed was being *in* love. Who doesn't miss that? That was the drug: Infatuation! Desire! Bliss! How did I go without it for so long? This is the greatest mystery of my life. How did I not shrivel up and die? Other women, they have children. They transfer their infatuation from their husbands to their kids. This is natural. I have witnessed this over and over with my friends. Babies are without sin. They are love magnets, cuteness machines to fixate on, blank slates upon which their mothers project the future. They provide infatuation and a lifetime of passion.

Baby daddies? Not so much.

I arrived in Paris. I was so jittery and nervous, I booked rooms in two different hotels under two different names. I can't explain why. What was I thinking? I wanted one room for us and one for myself. An emergency retreat, in case I felt the urge to flee. In case I, for whatever reason—guilt, nervousness, my own fear of looking older or of being rejected—could not allow myself to have what I wanted: Grant Hart.

I will not bore you with my preparations. The shopping, the gym workouts, the diets, the salon visits. If I could have found a nail salon selling aphrodisiac lacquers, I would have spared no expense.

I spent thousands of dollars pampering myself, making myself elegant and attractive. I bought one designer dress to show off my slim ankles and graceful calves and another to showcase my collar bones while hinting at the cleavage below. Then I began to worry about intimidating Grant. I bought ten pairs of designer jeans. New jeans, distressed jeans, blue jeans, black jeans, skinny jeans. I became exhausted. I broke down while having my hair colored. The colorist was my savior.

"Madame," she said, "you must hire a stylist. *C'est fini.*"

I did that. In the end, I wore lightly distressed jeans, a silk blouse, a string of pearls, and flats. "This is you, madame, trans-possessed from college," said Luc, my curiously fluent English-speaking stylist. "You must meet him in the daylight, so he can see your beauty is not based in shadows."

"I think it has to be night. *Tout le monde aime samedi soir,*" I sang, trying to convince myself.

"No, madame. Your allure will grow as you go into the evening."

"Maybe four o'clock?"

"*Bon!*"

The day before I was to meet Grant, Fatima texted me. I hadn't told my parents or my old friend Tabitha from school what I was doing. But for some reason I'd given my number to my hotel maid. I told you I was mad! I suppose that in recent months I had come to regard her as an ally, as someone I could trust. She had, after all, alerted me to the inquiries of Ayman's men. If they returned, I wanted to know.

They are looking for you!

Who?

The men who work for your husband. The man from the lobby. Also others.

Oh.

They searched your room. I tried to stop them. I told them it is private and it is locked. They just laughed and kicked the door in.

There was nothing there. Just my clothes and jewelry.

I know. But still.

I'm sorry if you were frightened.

They questioned me. Where is madame? Where did she go? Who does madame see? They said I was lying. The hotel director came. He asked them to leave. They asked him the same questions.

Thank you for telling me. I must go now.

I copied all the information I needed from my phone into a small notebook. I deleted all my apps and my texts. I hit reset for my phone and took out my sim card. I headed to Gare du Nord, the train station. I saw a woman laden with bags and a small child.

In my broken French, I asked if I could help her. "*Aidez-vous?*"

"*Oui, merci.*"

"*Ou allez, madame?*"

"*Berlin,*" she said.

I grabbed her rolling suitcase and hoisted a small knapsack over my shoulder. "*Allons-y,*" I said. Let's go.

As I accompanied her to the departure gate, I unzipped the front pocket on the knapsack and slid my phone into the bag. At the gate, she smiled at me and said, "*Merci.*"

"*De rien,*" I lied. It's nothing. But it wasn't. I prayed she would discover the phone when she was deep within

Germany's borders and discard it before my husband's men could track her down.

I went back to my hotel and checked out, then crossed the Seine to a new hotel. I put my sim card into my new phone and messaged Grant.

It's me. My phone broke. Here's my new number. I cannot wait to see you again.

His response was instant.

Me too.

CHAPTER 15

In which Lady Vanessa surveys her past and summons her courage

Lady Vanessa spent three more days in bed after Halloween. On the first day, she watched movies on the Hallmark channel. On the second day, she looked up the definition of addiction.

It was a noun. A thing. A state of being. She read essays on addiction. It was, one clever addict said, something you could have but not something you could possess. Instead, it possessed you. On the third day, at about 4 p.m., she got up and took a shower.

She recalled being a teenager in Bergen County, New Jersey. Her best friend was named Heather—such a romantic name! During the summer, Heather's older sister Alice would take them on a walk that would invariably end at a stationery store that sold Archie Comics and paperback books.

Lady Vanessa was known as Little Max at this time. She liked that name, except when a neighborhood know-it-all said, "How can you be small and maximum at the same time? It's an oxymoron!" Little Max didn't like the sound of an oxymoron. It sounded like acne medicine for stupid people.

Remembering this made Lady Vanessa laugh. She recalled how she and Heather would read the comics while Alice stood in front of a wire display carousel filled with books with women with long hair and dresses on the covers. When it was time to leave, they would buy an ice cream on a stick or sometimes a plastic tube of orange ice that she could squeeze out from the bottom.

By the end of the summer, however, all three girls would stand by the rotating wire book racks, reading about princes and ladies, earls and dames, and kings and commoners in England.

Soon she and Heather would go to read together without Alice. Eventually, she progressed from speed reading at the stationery store to weekly checkouts of Georgette Heyer and Barbara Cartland during high school.

In college, Maxine realized she was not a good close reader when it came to romances. She did not examine the text the way her professors did, looking for themes and tropes and symbolism.

She just liked a good story. A great story! She liked books that made her feel for the main characters, women who had to fight to live happily ever after. Was there any other point to life? To desire and be desired, to live with confidence and trust, to put fear in the rearview mirror of life and live joyfully with one man, all insecurities vanquished, because this is what love—true love—achieved in those stories: happiness, contentment, fulfillment, bliss.

Eventually, as she got older and the world of romance novels began to expand, she realized these tales of heartbreak, heroes, and the quest for happiness weren't just about damsels and princesses. Suffering wasn't reserved for royalty, the upper classes, and those who served them. They were for everyone. Maidens and charwomen. Firemen and Navy Seals. Werewolves and vampires.

Love, just like unhappiness, was for all.

During college, the books began to interfere with her schoolwork and friendships. Her roommates noticed her reading material. Some made comments. Feminists from the Women's Collective gave her looks or asked if she didn't have a problem with the gender roles in the books.

"Should I?" Maxine would say. Often the answer was yes, and she was lectured about the sexist subtext of her beloved stories. After a number of these encounters, Maxine got smart.

"It's just trashy fun," she started saying. "I like them because they're great, cheesy stories. Yes, sometimes they're absurd. I know they aren't politically correct, but they are sort of modern-day fairytales. With endings that leave you feeling good."

This was her attempt at having it both ways. She projected the idea that romances were silly and at the same time admitted her love for them. But it was an act. She never thought they were silly. Fun, yes. Escapist, yes. But silly? No, they were mesmerizing!

After college, she read alone. In private. She didn't want anyone to know. Not anyone at work. Not anyone anywhere. She knew people judged her. It was as if she read porn, something that people judged you unfavorably for.

As she remembered those feelings, she wondered if that was what junkies did. Cursed the dope and then kept shooting up in secret? There was a difference, though. Most junkies eventually, on some level, knew what they were doing was bad. They regretted their behavior. But Lady Vanessa had never felt that way. She felt inspired, moved, worried, thrilled, titillated, and ultimately happy when she read her stories. Life was hard. Life could be hell. But at the end, somewhere, there was security and kindness and love.

But maybe *that* was a drug. Maybe her daughter was right. Maybe she was an addict.

And right now, recently, she did feel bad. She was still embarrassed about Nelson Dodge. All the signs had been there! He was, as Helene Foxtrot-Mallory wrote of Malcomb Blazeman in her underground '70s classic *The Village People*, "camp as a row of tents." The poodle, his very tall friend who was obviously a drag queen, his perfectly coiffed hair, and his friends…the sleeveless button-down shirt Fabian Husk wore might as well have been a billboard: Gay Man Alert!

And she had ignored all the signs.

She cringed. Then she recalled the man from Grey's Plumbing.

Was she crazy?

Or just love crazy?

❦

Another day passed. She got out of bed, put on a simple dress, pulled her ringleted tresses back in a hefty ponytail, and dusted her face with some powder. She searched the internet, found the information she wanted, and left her apartment.

She walked four blocks to a church on Amsterdam Avenue. She felt strange going to a church. Even though she was a lapsed Jew who had married a lapsed Lutheran, this was alien territory. She had visions of crucifixes and pews with those knee rest things. When she arrived at the church, a sign directed her to the basement. That was a relief. She didn't want to deal with the hall of worship, with God, with any of this, really. Entering the basement hall, she thought she could be anywhere: the rec room in her apartment building's basement or a community center.

There were a dozen or so metal folding chairs arrayed in a semicircle and she took a seat. A tall, handsome man with too-long hair like a faded, decaying rock star was talking about how his wife had walked out on him.

"I've lost her," he said in the hoarse voice of a smoker. "She warned me. She told me she would if I didn't stop. I never believed her."

Lady Vanessa wondered if saying it aloud made it more real and more painful. She remembered Jacquelynn de la Pena's description of Thomas Riche IV in *An Embarrassment of Riches*: "He was a bon vivant who would cross the line over and over again, led by his demons, getting into fist-fights, crashing cars, spending nights in jail, and making bail. His mother said he put the pain in champagne."

Is that what this man was? She had no idea. He seemed sad. Thomas Riche IV had finally been forced to come to grips with his life when he woke up beside Kitty Getty, and she was stone cold dead. Fortunately, his first true love, Melanie Anderson, whose husband had been struck by lightning on the eighteenth hole at St. Andrews, helped him uncover the sinister plot by Kitty's stepbrother to make Thomas Riche IV the fall guy.

When she was called upon by the session leader, she said, "My name is Lady Van—no, actually, it's Maxine."

Two people in the circle, a rail-thin older man with a pock-marked face and a younger woman in a tank-top that showed off arms awash in tattoos, laughed.

"Whatever you're comfortable with," said the group leader, a stocky man with a warm smile and shaved head. "Welcome to our group."

"It's definitely Maxine."

"Hello, Maxine," said everyone in the room.

"Thanks. No, really, my legal name is Maxine. I enjoy being Lady Vanessa, but that's part of the problem."

She looked out at the room. Nobody said anything.

"It's a long story."

"We've got some time," murmured the leader.

"Let me start again. My name is Maxine. And I enjoy romance novels," she said. "And my problem, I think, is that I enjoy them maybe a little too much."

She paused. It was very quiet. The attendees were looking at her. "Have you ever had anyone come here addicted to books?"

"I don't think so," said the leader.

"We had a guy a few months back. He was hooked on porn," said the man who had laughed.

"That was online," said the tattooed young woman. "Videos online. He said he couldn't stop…you know."

"Oh, I can stop," Lady Vanessa said, her face flushing. All of a sudden, she wanted to leave. She felt embarrassed. "I can stop anytime. In fact, I already have. Sort of."

"Maxine, I'm really glad to hear that," said the session leader. "But I've said those exact words, 'I can stop anytime,' at least a hundred times. And I was wrong."

"Well, I really *feel* like I can stop. Anyway, it's just books."

"Porn is just pictures and videos," said the young woman. "But that guy we had here, man, he said he'd just spend hours yanking his junk. He said he couldn't sleep. Then he started watching at work and got caught. He got fired."

"Nobody is going to fire me. I don't have a job. And even if I did, I don't think I'd get fired for reading my stories. It's not like they're smut. I mean, some of them are. But most are not."

"*Fifty Shades of Lay*!" called the young woman. Lady Vanessa wondered if she was addicted to ink and needles.

"Mary, please," said the leader. "Maxine, why did you come here today?"

"My daughter put the idea in my head. But also, I want to change. This is so…this is embarrassing. I had a secret identity. I got carried away, I guess. I was pretending to be someone else, like a character from a book. And now I've met someone. I don't want him to think I'm a nutjob. A lot of people judge."

"For reading books?" said Mary.

"For reading romances. People can make you feel like you are part of a ghetto. Like it's déclassé."

"Of course it's classy! It's reading! I don't get it. You have my respect."

Maxine wondered if Mary was a distant relative of Magdalena. She nodded at the young woman. "Thank you. But it's more my behavior than the books. My daughter says I was lost in a fantasy. I guess I was."

"How do you feel now? Talking about this?" It was the leader.

"I don't know. Embarrassed? Foolish? A little crazy, but also a little relieved. It was me, but it wasn't me. I see that now. That's why I think I can stop."

"Stop reading?"

"Stop being this other person. Start being me."

"Is part of being you also reading books, Maxine?"

"I think so. But I need to separate from those books. I need to remember they are just a certain kind of entertainment. Not the gospel."

Nobody said anything.

Maxine looked out at the room. "I think I'm done," she said. "When do we hug?"

Not long before Thanksgiving, New York was caught in a rare November snowstorm, one of the few events that could silence the twenty-four-hour city. A foot of snow fell. Maxine knew that life would be suspended while the entire population of the city hunkered down in their isolated compartments. Tom—Mr. Miller—had been over with his sketch pad. She'd made dinner. He drew her portrait.

"Draw one of yourself," Maxine said. "You have a bunch of me. I want one of you."

"Me? I'm sick of drawing me! Who do you think I draw when I have no models around? Miller in the mirror! But okay, I'll do one from memory."

When he was done, he signed the bottom, tore the page from his sketchbook with a flourish, and handed it to Maxine. "For your approval."

Maxine studied the self-portrait. She remembered what Tom had said about noses. He hadn't spared himself in this rendition, bestowing upon himself a large, slightly hooked beak. It was a rugged honker, as he might say, recalling the kind of nose a beefy, charismatic mobster in a Hollywood movie might have. The rest of his features were exaggerated in the opposite direction. Shrunk. His handsome gray eyes reduced to dots at the bottom of a shrunken version of his prominent, rock-cliff of a forehead. She held the paper, staring at it, interpreting it. Was it a throw-away or an artful sight gag? A work of humor, a gesture, a statement. She felt a charge emanating from it. Did that even make sense? She smiled because even if it didn't, it did to her.

"Do you like it?"

"As a cartoon, a caricature, yes, very much. As a self-portrait, well, I miss your eyes. And you shrank your forehead to overstate your nose."

"That's an excellent appraisal. You should teach."

"May I keep it?" Maxine said, hoping he would see this request as the statement of desire it was.

But Mr. Miller didn't seem to notice. He clapped his hand to his forehead and said, "I forgot to take my medicine." Then he grabbed his pad and pencil and stood up. "Thank you for a wonderful evening."

Maxine wanted to say, "Stay a while," or "Come back. Let's watch the snow together and enjoy the quiet of the city." She wanted this funny, handsome, well-worn man to hold her. She wanted to kiss him. She thought he did too. But he left.

Maxine stood in her apartment, watching the snowflakes float through the beams of the streetlights. She thought about her books. They were off-limits. They were a link to Lady Vanessa. But what about having a Jane-a-Thon? Those predated Lady Vanessa. She didn't feel, given the circumstances, that it would be a violation of the unwritten laws of recovery. She went into her bedroom closet, parted the dozens of dresses and jackets that hung there, and surveyed a bookshelf with DVDs lining the back wall.

She had them all. Well, almost all, as "all" was a debatable number. There was no way she considered *Bride and Prejudice,* a modern Bollywood-style musical, or the 2003 abomination of the same name that was set in contemporary Utah, as part of the true Jane canon, although she did own both.

The same went for other updates, like the horribly titled *Pride and Prejudice and Zombies.* Her daughter Emma had raved about that movie and the title, but Maxine thought it was in bad taste. Nobody wrote movie-parodies called *The New Testament and Zombies.* Or *The Koran and Zombies.* Jane Austen didn't deserve that.

Maxine did not own the 1938 movie starring Welsh beauty Curigwen Lewis, who had a wry look that was becoming of Elizabeth Bennett, and Andrew Osborn, the first cinematic— and sadly disappointing—Mr. Fitzwilliam Darcy.

But she did have the DVD of the 1940 romance version starring Greer Garson as Elizabeth Bennet and Laurence Olivier as Mr. Darcy.

Sadly, she had yet to locate the 1949 TV episode from The Philco-Goodyear Television Playhouse series starring Madge Evans and John Baragrey or a copy of the 1952 TV series with Alan Badel and Jane Downs.

She did, however, own the 1967 version with Celia Bannerman and Lewis Fiander, the 1980 miniseries starring Elizabeth Garvie and David Rintoul, the 1995 series with Colin Firth and Jennifer Ehle, the glorious 2005 movie starring Keira Knightley and Matthew Macfadyen and the lack-luster 2014 series starring Luke McGibney and Jolie Lennon.

Also on the shelves were two versions of *Sense and Sensibility*, including the masterful production with Emma Thompson, Kate Winslet, and the divine Hugh Grant. And four versions of the brilliant *Emma*, that marvelous celebration and annihi-lation of matchmaking busybodies, and two versions each of *Mansfield Park, Northanger Abbey*, and *Persuasion*.

She stood in the closet and looked at her collection. Given the snowstorm, there was really only one viewing choice: to luxuriate in one of the long series, the box sets. But which one? What was the thing that she relished above all, besides the story, for they all told the same story? Was it the acting? The cinematography? The genteel costumes? Was it Elizabeth, that heroine among all heroines? "My little Lizzy," as her father calls her, who must live in dire uncertainty about her heart and her fate and endure not only the awful inher-itance laws of the time but the approaches of that dreadful parson? She was an inspiration, Elizabeth Bennett, Maxine thought. Our stand-in for Jane, the writer, the sufferer, the jester behind the book's opening sentence and that spiked each adaptation: *It is a truth universally acknowledged, that a sin-gle man in possession of a good fortune, must be in want of a wife.*

What a sentence! A brilliant, spellbindingly true-yet-false, ironic sentence, as Maxine knew too well. Her ex-husband did not, ultimately, want a wife. He wanted waitresses and bimbos; he wanted sex and to be left alone. And Nelson Dodge! He certainly did not want a wife. This was a false assumption and yet universally held. Who doesn't want a partner?

The further irony, as Maxine had to acknowledge, was the Austen book, and all its film adaptations were about how a single woman with few options—Elizabeth—should understandably be *in want of a man in possession of a good fortune*. And boy, did her love for Mr. Darcy amp up after she saw Pemberley, his grand estate.

And that is why, in the final analysis, Maxine had to admit that what truly drove her passion for this book and this movie was not just the witty and wise Elizabeth, but the flappable, decent, misunderstood, handsome, and beyond loaded Mr. Darcy. A sensible, patient alpha male in perfectly tailored clothing. A man who listens! A man who doesn't want the woman he loves to change. A man who looks great in wet clothing! Who admits to being awkward and refuses to deny his faults. Although, really, could a man as handsome and decent as Colin Firth have any faults?

She went back to the living room, a DVD box set in each hand: the one with Macfadyen and the one with Firth. She thought about watching one episode from each. No, she decided. That's what Lady Vanessa would do.

She pulled out the disc from the first episode of the Firth box and inserted it into the player. Then she put Tom's self-portrait by her side on the couch, picked up the remote control, sat back, pressed play, and sighed.

CHAPTER 16

In which the author briefly examines love and loss

That was a hard chapter to write.

Not because it dealt with heavy issues. Or because Lady Vanessa transforms, like some paranormal heroine, back into Maxine. No, the problem I faced was quite the opposite.

There was so much potential for the blackest, bleakest comedy to be launched in an Al-Anon meeting. In my initial outline for the book, I had her enraptured by the story of the man in recovery who pours his heart out about being left behind.

Naturally, Maxine's Lady Vanessa persona, the advisor of ardor and the lecturer of love, would resurface to bully her way into this poor man's life, encouraging him to fight for his true love. At her urging, he would wind up facing stalking charges. Or she could urge him to propose, and he does just that, oblivious to the fact she's on a date with another man, who proceeds to batter the lovelorn loser. Ah, so many potential setups for comedy.

But I seek the resurrection! I want to see Lady Vanessa—I still prefer that name to Maxine—to be happy. Just like I want to see me happy. Or wanted to see me happy.

Now, I'm not so sure. Not about Lady Vanessa. She must triumph! It's me I'm worried about.

I am in love, readers! I am enveloped, cocooned, swathed in bliss. Grant Hart!

Let me say it some more:

GrantHartGrantHartGrantHartGrantHartGrantHart GrantHart!

I am reborn a teenager. I'm crazy in love. Me! With a perfect match. A man with whom I am fully, 1,000 percent compatible—emotionally, sexually, and all the other 'ly's you can think of. And the tragedy is, I always was. Oh, I could scream at my damn mother and her "fully compatible" guilt trip.

And, if I'm honest, I should scream at myself too. I can't unload it all on my mother. I should have known better. By the time I was eighteen years old, I knew she'd been wrong about so many things. That dancing led to sex. That all Jews were rich. That sex before marriage was catastrophic. Why did I succumb to her "fully compatible" nonsense? I have no answer beyond wanting to be a dutiful daughter and wanting to trust in the wisdom of my elders; I really hoped they were right.

Like a character in one of Lady Vanessa's amnesia stories, years have passed between Grant and me. And yet...is it the absence that fuels us? Or has a great wound been healed by time? Or, I wonder as I gaze at Grant, is this just right? Just destiny?

Grant! He is older, thicker, and yet more handsome, more rugged, and just as kind.

We were both speechless when we met at Ile des Copains, the 150-year-old-restaurant I'd selected for its intimate booths. Any anxiety melted away instantly. The space between us dissolved from the moment of our first clench.

For hours, we barely lost physical contact. We held hands as we sat across from each other at dinner, our legs entwined below the table. When we walked, our arms locked, my body nestling into his as if magnetized. We never let go. Never. And when we fell together, finally alone, our lips endlessly teasing, nibbling, feasting, our bodies yearning, driving, melding, it was like reaching life's summit. The highest of glorious highs.

Even now, as he sleeps and I sit at the hotel room desk five feet away, I gaze at him and I feel alive and electric. I am so fucking happy, I feel drunk.

And then, like a drunk who has gone over the limit, I slide into misery.

What if this happiness ends?

What if I have put him in harm's way?

What if I have put myself in harm's way?

I try to dismiss these questions. I'm being paranoid. My husband would never harm me. I think of my phone traveling to Berlin, its pings hitting cell towers along the way, and my husband's men struggling to track them down and find me.

And failing.

CHAPTER 17

In which Lady Vanessa vanishes
and a son appears

Magdalena was worried.

In just a few weeks, Lady Vee had changed. Her voice was lower when she talked. Before, it was like she was somebody in a play or something. Now she didn't sound so special. The hoop skirts were gone in favor of jeans. Her lipstick was muted. She had painted over her Tiger Urine Moon Lust nail polish with a bland, tan lacquer. Even her name had changed. She was now Maxine.

Abandoning Lady Vanessa was difficult for Magdalena, who thought Lady Vee was a mad great name. Magdalena's hours had switched from Monday, Wednesday, and Friday to Tuesday and Thursday, which kind of sucked, because that meant less bank.

But what really worried her was that Lady Vee's mojo was gone. She had stopped lecturing about comportment and the other Five Cs of Romance. She rarely mentioned any of the lessons she'd learned from great authors and their valuable books.

And she stopped calling her Magdalena or her lady-in-waiting. Now it was just plain old Maggie. Like everyone else.

One of the girls back in Sunset Park—Iris, who had first tipped Maggie off to Dragon's Heart Nail Salon and the alleged aphrodisiacal powers of Tiger Urine Moon Lust—pronounced Lady Vee mentally ill as soon as she heard about Maxine's new manicure.

"That bitch is crazy!" cried Iris. "Even faded and chipped, that polish is like a porno-potion! She must be losing her mind or depressed."

Magdalena wondered about Lady Vee's mental health too. But the fact was, her boss didn't seem depressed. Quieter? Yes. More withdrawn? Yes. More relaxed? Totally! Her heated lectures about romance were few and far between now. Maxine was more interested in baking and cookbooks than reciting chapter and verse of her romance books. And any critical remarks about Maggie's healthy appetite had come to a halt, which was kind of nice.

What really worried Maggie was that Lady Vee—Maxine!—was obsessed with the older gent next door, who was now a frequent guest at Lady Vanessa's apartment. They would sit and drink tea together. Sometimes Lady Vee—Maxine!—would invite her to join them and listen while Mr. Miller described his travels.

That's all the guy seemed to do. Take trains through Europe. Eat in India. Dance in some African country Maggie had never heard of. Or teach drawing in some unknown college in Illinois or Minnesota where it was a million degrees below zero.

Lady Vee listened to all his stories as if they were the most fascinating things she'd ever heard. But it reminded Maggie of the docu-bores on public television, shows that were the opposite of reality TV.

Still, Maggie was happy for her boss if she was happy. And to be honest, she was sometimes glad Lady Van—Maxine!— had lost her passion for romances. It was dizzying trying to remember all the authors' names and their characters and plots and lessons of each book. But now Maggie had to face facts. Maxine's crush seemed destined to leave her lady-in-waiting doing just that: waiting.

Mr. Miller was way older than Nelson Dodge, and as she saw it, that meant any wingman he had was likely to be the same age. Months ago, Lady Vee had assured her that whoever she hooked up with would likely have a butler or footman who would be a match for Maggie. And that sounded perfect. But the likelihood of Mr. Miller, who drew cartoons for a living and didn't seem to have major bank, having a friend like Nelson's mega-hot buddy Fabian seemed low. She needed advice.

"Your mom has mad changed," she said on the phone to Emma.

"I know! Thank you for all your help."

"I didn't do nothing. I'm trying to figure out what's going on."

"My mother hasn't really been normal since you met her, Maggie, as you know. I'm thrilled that she seems to be getting back to our current century and being Maxine again."

"Yeah, well. I called because, you know, I wanted to ask if I should be worried."

"About what?"

"My hours. And your mom's, like, new jam. She almost seems, like, depressed or something compared to how she used to roll."

"That's so funny, Maggie. Her old jam wasn't good. She was living in a make-believe world. But I know she adores you and wants you to work—just fewer hours."

"I hear you," said Maggie, although she really didn't. "Okay. Thanks."

Magdalena hung up. She took a deep breath. She was just going to have to go with the flow.

Upon entering Lady Vee's building later that afternoon, she found Mr. Miller waiting for the elevator. He was talking to a tall, strapping young man with a mountain man beard and a backpack. He was wearing a pair of Yeezy Boost sneakers and had a pair of expensive-looking headphones cradling his massive neck. He looked like a hip-hop lumberjack.

"Maggie," Mr. Miller greeted her. "So nice to see you. This is my son, Trevor."

Immediately, Magdalena's attitude toward Mr. Miller warmed. "Yo, Mr. Miller," she said, offering a fist bump to the younger man. "I didn't know you were a baby daddy to a masterpiece. I thought you just drew them!"

Mr. Miller let out a big laugh, and Trevor smiled and returned the bump.

"Nice to meet you, Maggie," he said.

"Magdalena is the close associate of my friend Maxine."

During the elevator ride, Maggie tried not to hyperventilate or stare at Trevor. This was even better than a wingman! Mr. Miller had a son who looked like a white, chunky version of that basketball player with a huge holy man beard whose name she could never remember.

He's perrrrrfect, she thought to herself.

Then she thought the unthinkable. The subject Lady Vee had lectured her about months ago about being taboo.

She thought, *This dude is double-wedding material!*

Maggie knew this was wrong. Like a violation of an unwritten commandment. But how could she resist? If things could work out for Maxine and Mr. Miller, why not her and Trevor? She would have to figure out how to run this idea by Lady Vee. Mentioning it now might push Her Ladyship off the deep end.

They got off the elevator. Mr. Miller and Trevor stopped in front of their apartment.

"Please give Maxine a warm hello from me," Mr. Miller said.

"Nice to meet you, Maggie," Trevor said, offering her a fist bump.

"Bam!" Magdalena said, flashing a hundred-watt smile as she returned the bump. Maxine was in the kitchen making brownies when Maggie waltzed in, intoxicated by her discovery.

"Lady Vee, Lady Vee! I mean, Maxine! I got big news."

"What is it?"

"Maybe you already know."

"I can't know if I already know until you tell me."

"About Mr. Miller and his son?"

"*His son?!*"

"I guess you don't."

"Tell me."

"It's nothing really. I just rode up in the elevator with him and his son, Trevor."

"His son Trevor," Maxine repeated dumbly.

"That's how he introduced him. Trevor. Trev! I guess they look alike, but his son is way taller and way hotter. No offense, Lady Vee. Sorry! I mean, Maxine."

"Is he there now?"

"Trevor? Yeah. He had a backpack with him. The dude looks rugged. Except no hiking boots. He had Yeezys. Those jams cost like exponential Benjamins."

"Are you talking about his footwear? Are those some kind of sneakers?" asked Maxine, although she didn't care about the answer.

She could feel Lady Vanessa creeping back into her soul. She wanted to castigate Maggie for her lack of decorum, for fawning over someone she knew nothing about. She also wanted to march over to Mr. Miller's apartment and demand to know why he had never mentioned a son. What was he hiding? Did he have a wife too?

Maxine undid her apron. "Can you take the brownies out for me?" she asked Maggie. "I just remembered. I have to go meet someone."

❦

The session in the church basement helped. First, she talked about her stories and how well she was doing keeping her alter-ego—"this other side of me, this romance monster"—in check. She got to talk about Mr. Miller. About how she was fixated. About how it was awkward. How today, when she found out his son was visiting, a son he had never mentioned, she was furious even though she really had no right to be. They were just getting to know each other. Still, she was worried.

"We live on the same floor. What if things go wrong?" she wondered. "Or should I just worry about things going right?"

She was too embarrassed to say what she was really worried about: sex and rejection. About it not clicking. About bodies and awkwardness. About not passing muster.

"How much older is he?" asked Mary.

"About twelve or fifteen years."

"You got nothing to worry about."

"How do you know?"

Mary's eyes narrowed on Maxine. It was a look of critical appraisal. "You're in good shape. He's thanking God you'll even look at him."

Two men in the room laughed.

Maxine felt herself blushing. "Thank you. But I'm not quite sure that's the case."

"Totally," said Mary. "Count on it."

Maxine returned home to find Mr. Miller and Trevor sitting in her kitchen. Her brownies were on the table, and Maggie was making coffee.

"There she is!" Mr. Miller said. "Maxine, I hope you don't mind us dropping by. I wanted to make sure to introduce you to my son, Trevor. Trevor, this is my friend Maxine, who I told you about."

"Welcome to New York, Trevor. How long are you here for?"

"A couple of days. I just decided to surprise Dad with a drive-by visit. Then we may hit the road."

"Oh, really? A father and son road trip? How fun!"

"Visiting relatives," Mr. Miller said. "Trevor lives outside Seattle, so I want to show him off. Maybe convince him to move this way."

"You should think about it," Maggie said. "Scientists think there's a massive earthquake coming over there."

"We try to live in denial," Trevor said.

"So does his dad," Mr. Miller said. "I worry about that too."

"No wonder pot's legal over there," Maggie said. "I'd need weed just to stay calm about that shit."

Trevor laughed. "That's funny. Is she always this funny?"

Maxine smiled. "Usually."

"No," Maggie contradicted her boss dramatically. Then she said, "I'm way funnier."

Everyone laughed. But beneath the mirth, Maxine was thinking about the prayer that her meeting group shared in the church basement. The one that asked for serenity.

⚬⚭⚬

As the day approached for Mr. Miller and Trevor's departure, Maxine grew worried. Tom—Mr. Miller had asked her to call him by his first name because "Mr. Miller makes me feel old, and that runs counter to the anti-aging effect you have on me"—continued to visit her daily.

He would bring over the *New York Times* and complain about events in Washington, and then he would ask her for help with the crossword puzzle. He would reminisce about his travels. He would talk about Trevor, which is how Maxine learned that Trevor had asked Maggie to accompany him to a hip-hop show in Brooklyn.

"Oh, dear," Maxine said.

"What?"

"I think Magdalena has a bit of a crush on your son. I hope it doesn't end in tears."

Tom also brought over a sketch pad and drew Maxine as she baked.

"Cartooning is seasonal for me," he said, explaining why he was in her kitchen, not looking for work near the Central Park Zoo. "Nobody wants to pose when the weather drops under fifty-five degrees. And believe me, nobody wants to draw either."

The day before he left, he showed her the finished work. It wasn't a cartoon or a caricature. It was a detailed, nuanced portrait.

"That's very flattering," Maxine said. It was. Her nose did not dominate her face, her brow was wide and strong, with a wisp of hair falling on it. She looked, she guessed, handsome.

"Yes, it's not bad."

"Not bad?"

"I feel like I've missed something. The true beauty of your eyes. I'll have to try again. I remember when I first met you, you were hiding them behind tons of makeup. I thought, what a sin!"

Maxine looked down at her apron. "Thank you. I was… confused."

"I know. Your daughter told me."

"She did?"

"Just once. We rode the elevator together and walked to the subway. She said you were struggling but that you were really a lovely woman."

"She was right, I was struggling."

"And you were—are—a lovely woman."

The oven timer beeped. The tea kettle whistled. It was a perfect storm of kitchen hell.

"Thank you," Maxine said, rushing to quiet things. "That's so kind of you to say."

But the spell was broken.

After six weeks, that was as close as he had ever come to making a pass at her.

When he left, she went to a meeting and shared the story.

"He knew me when I was this other person. And he still likes me," she said. "It's really hard to believe. To accept. I'm so grateful, even though he hasn't made a pass at me."

"Maxine," said the group leader for the day. "I think maybe that was a pass."

That evening, Tom stopped by again. To invite her to dinner.

"I'm happy to cook," Maxine said, trying not to break into a triumphant smile.

"No, no," said Tom, "How many times have you cooked for me or fed me cookies or pies? It's time for my treat."

They went to a Thai place. Tom had switched planes in Bangkok on a cheap ticket to India. Maxine had seen *The King and I.* That was their collective knowledge of Thailand. They laughed at their shared ignorance.

"But the entire Upper West Side has become amateur experts in Thai food." Tom laughed. "I'll tell you what I'm not an expert at: looking for work."

"Me, too. Emma keeps telling me I need to find a job. I don't feel like going back to teaching."

"That's funny. It is absolutely time for me to teach again. I've been buried in applications all day," he said. "I'm tired of beating the pavement and freelancing. I could use some stability."

"Professor of Cartooning?"

"Drawing. There are plenty of colleges around. But my resume isn't exactly stellar. It feels like a long shot with some of these jobs. A very long shot."

Maxine asked how long he'd be gone. And Tom sighed.

"I'm not sure. You know I'm subletting the apartment, Maxine. You must know the Lavers."

"I steered clear of them. They used to complain when Emma was little and was noisy on the stairs or made a sound in the hall."

"They just hiked my rent by five hundred dollars."

A dark thought washed over Maxine. Was this courtship nothing more than a premeditated land-grab?

"When did you find out about the rent?"

"This morning. She sent an email."

Maxine exhaled in relief.

"It's kind of a shock. I guess I'll deal with it when I get back, which should be after the New Year."

She wanted to say something. To put herself, her feelings, out there.

"I'm sure it will work out. It has to. I…"

"That's the way I feel."

He moved his hand across the table and placed it on hers.

TRANSLATOR'S NOTE #7

In the upcoming chapter, incredibly, the ostensible author, Aisha Benengeli makes an apparent authorial misstep. As you will see, she abandons her pseudonym and refers to herself as Rana, the very name I discovered and revealed in my previous note. The question for readers and translators alike is whether this usage was intentional or a mistake. Personally, I believe it is a reflection of the torment and pressure she felt as she rushed to complete her manuscript. She appears to be faithfully recording a conversation when she lets her real identity slip. Part of me believes the shrewd author, unburdened by pressures, surely would have edited the exchange, changing Rana to Aisha. Indeed, the entire book has been cloaked in anonymity.

But another part of me wonders about her state of mind and her presence of mind. She is worried. Nervous. She feels she is in danger. Does she have the time or the focus to properly edit? Maybe she no longer cares. And the ruse that drove her at the beginning of the book, the cloaking of her identity, has changed in importance. Maybe she wants to be seen, heard, identified. Especially if she is worried about being silenced.

And so, in what follows, I have taken no liberties. I present what I was presented with, my only wish to serve the author, her text, and the reader as faithfully as I can.

CHAPTER 18

In which love is celebrated— and turns to grave danger

Finally!

Holding hands. So simple. So intimate. Not as fun as a kiss, but sometimes far less complicated and therefore more reassuring. A chaste kiss, after all, can be a contradiction in terms to the person on the receiving end. Maxine is in love and is loved! Could I have it any other way? I suppose so. Yes, I could have put it off.

Lady Vanessa could have encountered gag after gag. She could have visited a fortune teller and fought with the charlatan over her supposed future. She could have attended a speed dating night. She could have landed a job as a romantic advice column for a hipster blog. A photograph of her birdcage hoop skirt could have made her a national figure of mockery on Twitter. But no! She deserves love, just like we all do.

Just like I do.

And so, while Grant Hart slept—I actually think of his name as a chant now, a mantra: *GrantHartGrantHartGrantHart*—I sat in bed, listening to his light snore, and wrote about love. Arranging Maxine's future, trying to leave her in good shape, and assuring she has her happily-ever-after.

Mine?

I hope so and I fear not.

We are a perfect union, Grant Hart and I. I won't bore you with our bliss, the warmth, the passion, the laughter, the tears, the raw sex, the intimate sex, the improvisational sex, the intense contentment and fulfillment, our eyes and bodies in lockstep.

After our first week together, I stepped off cloud nine for a brief second. I looked at my phone, something I hadn't done all week, and remembered I had not given my new number to my parents. I called.

"Hello?"

"Hi, Daddy. It's me."

"Good God! Rana! Where are you?"

"I'm abroad. In Europe."

"Ayman has been looking for you. He sent his men here. For three days, they lived with us. Answering our phones, demanding to see our emails. They had guns!"

"Put the phone on speaker!" I heard my mother say. Then she was in my ear, full blast. "What have you done, Rana? These men threatened us!"

"*What?*"

"They said you have fled."

"I went on a trip...to see some friends."

"Ayman is furious. He suspects you of being unfaithful. Of disgracing him."

"Ayman has disgraced me. I am not a piece of chattel! He doesn't own me."

"A husband has the right to know where his wife is."

"Then I am no longer his wife."

"Oh God!" my mother wailed to my father. "She will kill us all!"

"I will call Ayman. Don't worry."

A new voice entered the fray. "Is madame okay?" It was Gamal, the family cook.

"Yes, yes, Gamal!" my father said. "Thank you. Madame is just a little upset."

"A *little* upset?" screeched my mother. "Please, Gamal. Some water."

"Yes, madame."

"Rana," my father said. "Ayman is very powerful. You must be careful."

"Daddy," I said. "Pack your bags. You must go to New York. You can stay at my apartment there."

"Why? What is going on?"

"You know what's going on. They're threatening you. You need to leave. I'm very sorry about this. I handled this very badly, but I had no idea he'd react this way."

"What way should he react?" shouted my mother. "When a man's wife disappears, how is he supposed to react?"

"Not by threatening you, Mama! Or Daddy. Or me!"

"Oh my God! Oh my God!"

"Your water, madame." I pictured Gamal, his somber face wrinkled with concern, offering a glass of water on a serving tray with a napkin beside it. It was time to make my getaway.

"I'll call you back. I love you both!"

I wanted to call Ayman right away. I got online and found an internet service that let me route a call anonymously. I had no intention of giving him a number that would divulge my location.

"Abboud here," he answered.

"It's me."

"Where are you, Rana?"

"I'm in the land of the free," I said, wanting him to think I was in the U.S.

"Who are you with?"

"That's not important. What is important is what I have decided: I cannot be with you. We are over. I want a divorce."

"That is not acceptable. You are my wife, and I have a reputation."

"I'm sorry, but I can't be with you."

"Who is he?"

"Who is who?"

"The man you are with."

"Who said I'm with a man?"

"I do."

"This has to do with one man: you. The man I am not with and cannot be with."

"Because I sell weapons?"

"Yes. And you lied to me."

"If I had told you I sold them—"

"Then I would have never given you a second look."

"Ah."

"And you've been bothering my parents. Leave them alone. They have nothing to do with this. This is my decision. You and I are finished. I'll have my lawyer file papers."

"Don't do that. This must be private. I have a reputation!"

"The only one who cares about your reputation is you. People get divorced all the time for many reasons. We are, it turns out, fully incompatible. Here: I divorce thee, I divorce thee, I divorce thee."

"If your lawyer breathes a word of this to anyone, it will be very bad. Do I make myself clear?"

"Ayman, your lawyers are just as likely to talk as mine are. More so, because my lawyers work for a client nobody cares about. I'm an obscure writer, if that. I can only promise you my own discretion."

I hung up the phone. Grant was stirring.

GrantHartGrantHartGrantHartGrantHart, I whispered to myself.

I sent my parents two tickets to New York. They refused to leave their home. I spent a week with Grant, alternating between the soothing heaven of his touch and the hell of anxiety.

I had to go back to get my parents, to make sure they would be okay. I would see about hiring a security firm to watch their house. I would find a lawyer. We would call Ayman. I would work out a settlement. I didn't need much—I had money and jewelry socked away. Grant and I could live in my apartment in New York. I had kept it even after I married.

GrantHartGrantHartGrantHartGrantHart.

I flew back and had a security guard meet me at the airport. He was a big, strapping man, a former Army captain named Ahmed. He drove me to the hotel. He asked for a chair, planted it outside my suite, sat down, and said, "I will be here twelve hours a day. My relief will be here at six. His name is also Ahmed. That is why we are A&A Security."

I had room service deliver dinner. Then I placed an order from the website at Habibi's Couture in Alexandria for a rush delivery. I told Ahmed to tell Ahmed that a package would arrive tomorrow. It was late and I was exhausted, but I couldn't sleep. My Grant Hart chant couldn't soothe what ailed me.

I was frightened.

I turned to Lady Vanessa—I mean, Maxine—for distraction and comfort.

CHAPTER 19

In which a mystery ends
and a new one begins

Life in New York had a way of speeding up for Christmas and then lulling into the holiday week. Maxine continued her Jane-a-thons. She went to meetings. She attended an aerobics class at a gym on Broadway. It felt good to move, and it even felt good to ache the next day. Maxine vowed to bake less and dance more in the new year. Did Tom dance? She felt certain he did.

That dinner with Tom had motivated her to move. Reminded her she had a body. His hand, that big, graceful center of his art, enveloped hers. And she remembered the electricity of skin. He pulled her hand to his lips and kissed it. Maxine couldn't remember anyone ever doing that before. Then he leaned across the table and kissed her on the lips.

It was gentle. At first, Maxine resisted the impulse to kiss him back deeply, fiercely. But she had resisted so much for so long. She put one hand behind his head; the other stroked his face. They were in public, snogging like teenagers! It was thrilling. She pulled back.

"Maybe we should get the check," she said.

They went home to her apartment, the better to avoid Trevor (and possibly Magdalena; the two had been spending time together, so much so that Maxine had issued her charge a pre-emptive warning: "If you mention a double wedding in my presence, you will be fired.").

She led him to her bedroom. She left the lights off. They tumbled onto the bed. They held each other. They kissed. Love can do many things, Maxine thought, but it can't make disrobing any easier. Clothes came off awkwardly, comically, stubbornly. And finally, they were naked and together.

They were, if not one, then a number very close to it.

❦

A card arrived. Tom had drawn a portrait of himself wearing enormous sunglasses. Etched in the lenses were the words "Coming Soon: Jan. 5."

The next day he called.

"It's eighty-three degrees here and sunny, and there's no place I'd rather be than New York," he said.

"Okay, I'll trade you."

"If you're not there, the deal's off."

"That's sweet."

"It's not sweet. It's true. Although Trevor doesn't concur. He's moving here."

"Oh." A sense of dread rose in her stomach.

"You're thinking of Maggie?"

"Yes. How can I not? She was here yesterday—cleaning when she wasn't mooning."

"Trevor swears there's been no intimate contact."

"Trevor is young and foolish. Being intimate doesn't just mean sex. Words are intimate. Shared experiences are intimate, especially with someone like Magdalena. Trevor included her in his life. I think that's rare for her."

"Well put. I always admired seeing the two of you out together."

Maxine cringed. He had seen her—Lady Vanessa, really—out with Maggie.

"That wasn't exactly me, you know."

"Yes. But still. You seemed like a team."

"Tom," she said. She had to ask. "What do you see in me? I was practically deranged three months ago."

"I see what the world sees. A beautiful woman with grace, humor, and kindness who laughs at my drawings and makes me happy. You had a…I don't what to call it. An episode. A break. You think I've always been the guy I am now? Call me old and foolish, but I think you're gorgeous, funny, and kind. I'm dying to see you."

"That's foolish?"

"No. Sorry. That's wise."

"How's Miami?"

"Fabulous in its cluelessness. What made it will destroy it. The proximity to the ocean."

"Yes. I'm sure the beach is partly why Trevor loves it. Wait till the brutal summer hits. Or hurricane season. Will you ask him to call Maggie?"

"Why are you so concerned about her?"

"Back when I was…not well…I promised her that if I met my prince, he'd likely have a gentlemen-in-waiting or a sidekick who'd be a match for her. Please ask Trevor to treat her with kindness. I'm sure he will. But Maggie bought into a fantasy I was selling."

"We all buy into fantasies."

"Yes. But not all fantasies become real."

"True."

"I'm very real now, Tom. I was in a fantasy before. But not anymore."

"I know. That's why I'd rather be in New York."

He came back. He got a job offer. Then he got another. One was out of town. In the Berkshires, tenure track. She lay awake weighing her responses. He should take it. He should commute. Work Monday to Thursday and then come home for long weekends. He could even move in with her. He should take the local job and keep his apartment. He should take the local job and move in with her. She would say nothing. She would offer her apartment.

In the morning, she felt his breath tickling her nape as he murmured that he would take the local job.

"Wonderful." This was pillow talk she wanted to hear.

"You approve?"

"Yes."

"It's a bad career move, but a good life move."

"I think so. The life move, I mean. Who knows what the local job will lead to? Could be even better."

"Better than this?"

He pulled her closer.

CHAPTER 20

In which a sudden and fraught farewell is issued

Dear Reader! I am so sorry! I have to stop here. I am very scared. Last night, Ayman called. He said this was my last chance. No, actually, he made a demand using the word "rapprochement," which is French for "working it out." Otherwise, he said cryptically, I "would face a dire existential crisis."

"That sounds like a threat, Ayman," I said. "I'm recording this conversation."

I wasn't. But I wish I had been.

He hung up. I sat staring into space for a moment, unable to focus. Then I resolved to go through with my plan.

Later, in the small hours of the night, I awoke to an argument outside my suite. I heard men shouting. Insults and threats were exchanged. And then it stopped. Had I dreamt it? It felt very real.

I'm frightened. For myself. For my parents. For my one and only GrantHartGrantHartGrantHart. Does Ayman know about him? I'll stop the manuscript here with Lady Vanessa—Maxine—in love! With a good man! That makes me happy.

And Magdalena? I almost forgot! Trevor has convinced her to take a course in computer coding. I have doubts about everything, but not about Maggie. She is young and on her way. And soon, I will be too. In a few moments, I will hit print and leave this book in trusted hands. I pray it will see the light of day. I pray I will see the light of day too.

Who knows if I'll ever have the opportunity to write, to dream, to love again? My mind races. I plan an escape. I summon my love. The thing I want most in this life or any other.

GrantHartGrantHartGrantHartGrantHartGrantHart.

Goodbye.

TRANSLATOR'S NOTE #8:
A POSTSCRIPT

*That is how Rana Abboud has ended her novel. But it does not fully
end her story.*

Disturbed by the final events in The Seductive Lady Vanessa
of Manhattanshire—*a veritable literary SOS—I knew I had to act.*

*Just as Rana had, I called A&A Security in Cairo and arranged
to be picked up at the airport. I flew to Cairo the next day. A tall, burly
man in a safari suit was holding a card bearing my name.*

"Ahmed?" I asked.

"At your service, madame!"

I had him drive me to Alexandria.

"You may be wondering why I hired you," I said.

*"Yes, but part of our service offers discretion. We don't believe in
pressuring our clients. Perhaps you just wanted a driver you could
depend on to deliver you to your destination."*

"I'm running an investigation into someone you know."

"Yes?"

"Rana Abboud."

*I could see from my vantage point in the back seat that his face
tightened for a second.*

"Rana Abboud," he repeated.

"A former client."

*"I can neither confirm nor deny any relations with any alleged
clients. If someone asked me about you, I would say the same thing."*

"I have written proof she hired you," I said. "I would like to know what happened."

"Who are you working for?"

I told him, as briefly as possible that I was researching Rana's life in an effort to finish a book she had been working on.

"Nothing happened. She disappeared on me."

"She disappeared on you? While you were protecting her? That sounds rather odd."

"I believe she wanted to be lost. She began acting very strangely. Early in the morning, she asked me to go down to the lobby to pick up a package with the concierge. I wondered why she didn't have a bellboy pick it up, but I went.

"Then, she summoned the cleaning maid. That was the only visitor. And two hours later, she asked me to go get another package. But there was nothing at the desk. And when I returned, she was gone, the door to her suite was wide open. On her bed was a note in a round, feminine script that said, 'Ahmed, thank you for your help.' There was no sign of struggle. Her purse and computer were missing. I assumed she left of her own accord. And later I confirmed that."

"When the maid came, did she leave empty-handed?"

"I don't recall. I think she might have had a bag. Yes, I think she did."

"Now tell me about the men who came in the night."

"That was my partner. I was off duty. We work six to six, twelve-hour shifts. But two men showed up, guns drawn. They demanded to see Madame Abboud. My partner pointed to the security camera in the hallway and told them to smile for the camera. 'You don't want to shoot me on videotape,' he told them. 'That's sloppy work.' They left. I arrived for my shift, and after about five hours on the job, she was gone."

"Did you look at the security footage to see her leaving the suite?"

"I did. It was very surprising."

"How so?"

"A woman walked out of the suite in a burqa."

"Ah," I said, thinking this was the item she mentioned ordering from Habibi's Couture, for I was certain she would never otherwise own such a garment.

"She was carrying a purse and bag. She looked completely anonymous."

"Did you see the tape of the men who came in the middle of the night?"

"I did. I asked for a copy, but hotel security refused. They would only share if there was a formal criminal investigation. I was in a jam. I guarantee my clients' anonymity. How could I go to the police?"

"What answer did you come up with?"

"I did nothing."

"Nothing? A woman disappears after men with guns show up. And you do nothing?"

"She paid a retainer."

"And that's how you repaid her?"

"I called her husband's office. I left my number. I said I thought I might be of help. He never responded."

"And the police? After her parents vanished, did you approach them? I believe, according to reports, that they disappeared around the same time."

"I did. They took my statement, but I never heard anything. The case remains unsolved."

"What do you think happened?"

"Either she and her parents were captured, or they went into hiding."

"Again, what do you think happened?"

"I believe they are buried in the desert or became shark chum. Her husband didn't seem to give a damn about her."

We rode in silence. He dropped me at the Four Seasons Grand Plaza in Alexandria, the place that Rana had last called home. I checked into my room on the seventeenth floor. I looked out at the rolling ocean below. It was a spectacular view. The sky was cloudless and blue. I was exhausted from my flight, and the conversation with Ahmed left me utterly crushed.

The next day, I set out to find Fatima, the hotel maid Rana Abboud mentioned in the manuscript. Convinced that hotel management would never help me locate a staffer if they knew I was investigating the whereabouts of a missing guest, I went up to the nineteenth floor and approached a maid pushing a trolley of linens down the corridor. I told her I was from New York and that I was looking for a cleaning woman on the staff named Fatima. I had a gift for her from a former hotel guest. I said I believed she worked on this floor.

The woman said Fatima worked in a wing on the opposite side of the hotel. *"Are you sure she didn't mean Rashida?"* she said with a laugh. *"That's my name."*

I gave her five dollars and thanked her.

I went to the east wing of the hotel. I found Fatima as she was locking up a suite. She was a small woman of about thirty. I introduced myself, telling her I was a book translator and that, as strange as it might sound, I had flown from New York to see her.

"Me? You flew all the way to see me?" The idea made her laugh nervously. I'm sure it seemed preposterous. She had never heard of me. She knew no one in New York.

"I'm working on a project involving someone you know," I said. *"We have, in a sense, someone in common. Our friend Rana Abboud."*

I realized I was stretching the truth a bit. But I didn't want Fatima to think I was aligned with Ayman.

Fatima's eyes narrowed at the mention of Rana's name. She looked down the corridor in both directions and took a deep breath.

"Is there somewhere you'd be more comfortable talking?" I said. "I'm staying at the hotel. We can go to my room."

"That would be against hotel rules."

"When do you end your shift?"

"At three."

I picked her up that afternoon in a taxi outside the employee entrance.

"My cousin has a cafe not far from here. We can go there and talk," she said, instructing the driver.

At the cafe, we ordered coffee and pastry.

"Rana Abboud wrote a book."

"I know. She was always writing."

"I received a manuscript in the mail. It had been found in an Yves Saint-Laurent shoulder bag. The souk merchant said he believed it came indirectly from a hotel worker in Alexandria."

"Why do you want to know about Mrs. Abboud?"

"The book I was sent was very, very good. I don't know if you looked at the manuscript, but even though it doesn't have Rana Abboud's name on it, it is clearly written by her. And of course, Rana Abboud has disappeared. Readers will want to know what happened to her, and I certainly want to know. I hoped you would help me fill in the blanks about Rana's last days at the hotel. Did she give you a copy of the book?"

"Yes."

"Yes, what?"

"*Yes, I will help you. And yes, she gave me a bag. Inside were many pages. I guess it was the book you mention. I didn't read it. There was also a white envelope. Inside was five hundred dollars and a short note. She said she was in fear of her life. That she believed her computer had been hacked, and she had destroyed it in the night and thrown the parts out of the window.*

"*She said she was running out of time, and she asked me to take care of her manuscript. She hoped she would come and reclaim it one day soon. She thanked me and said she was sorry for causing me any trouble.*

"*I took the bag home. Two days later, however, the men came to the suite, men who said they worked for Ayman Abboud, Madame Rana's husband. They demanded to know where she was and what she had left behind. They threatened me. If they found out I was lying, they said, they would kill me and my daughter.*

"*I couldn't believe they mentioned my daughter. How did they know about her? I am just a hotel maid. I am of no importance. I went home. My cousin lives across the street from us. I brought her the bag. 'Please,' I said, 'I must ask you a favor. Get rid of this bag for me, quickly! The woman who gave it to me is in trouble, and now I'm in trouble. Sell it, or burn it. Don't tell me anything, but make it go far away from here.' She said not to worry. She admired the bag and said she knew someone who was going to Cairo. He would sell the bag there.*"

Fatima looked me in the eyes. "*I'm so sorry. But I was so scared. I betrayed Madame Rana. But what could I do?*"

I touched her hand in sympathy and told her that I knew Rana would understand. "*She would have done the exact same thing,*" I said. "*She would understand the great love and obligation you had to your child. And, luckily, by some miracle, the book is with me now. I will see it is published.*"

"What do you think happened to her?"

"I don't know. You said the men asked you where she was?"

"Yes."

"But they came two days after she disappeared? You're sure?"

"Yes."

I thought about this. For the first time, the sense of anguish that had gripped me since landing in Cairo eased slightly. If Ayman's men had come looking for her, if they were actively searching for her, could she have gotten away? Did that mean Ayman's denials of involvement were true?

I had one more stop to make in Alexandria. I wanted to see the home of Rana Abboud's parents. They lived in Kafr Abdu, a posh neighborhood not far from elegant Allenby Gardens. The house was large and sturdy. And when I rang the doorbell, a woman answered.

"Mrs. Hamdy?" I asked. That was, of course, Rana's maiden name. I was guessing that such a stately home would have stayed within the family.

"Yes?"

I told her I was visiting from New York and that I was working on a book project that involved Rana. I hoped to ask her a few questions.

She seemed hesitant.

"I realize this is a painful matter for you, but I may have some information of interest."

She invited me in, and we sat in a spacious living room that hadn't been updated since the 1970s.

"Gamal!" she called out. *"Please bring us some tea."*

She told me her name was Anat Hamdy. Her husband was Rana's uncle, the brother of Rana's father Rahim. He was a professor of mathematics at Alexandria University. They had moved into the house one year ago.

"*The court decided that my husband was Rahim's closest relative and awarded us the house. Luckily, the rest of the family was agreeable. It is such a tragedy.*"

"*What do you think happened?*"

"*We are at a loss. Rahim had told my husband that Rana wanted to leave Ayman and that men working for Ayman had threatened him. There had been a home invasion. But the police say there is no evidence of sinister behavior. Ayman is very powerful. Very rich. And Egypt, as you know, suffers from corruption.*"

An elderly man dressed in a crisp white kaftan brought a tray of tea and biscuits.

"*Thank you, Gamal,*" *Mrs. Hamdy said.* "*Gamal was the last person to see my brother. He worked for them. Gamal, this is Ms. Oona. She is working on a project about Rana.*"

Gamal gave a slight bow.

"*Yes, madame. I served dinner to Madame Rana's parents. I cleaned up and asked if they required my services. Then I bid them goodnight. In the morning, I brought their tea upstairs. Their bedroom door was open, the bed still made from the day before. They were gone.*"

"*And Rana?*" *I asked.* "*Was she here then?*"

"*I did not see her, madame.*"

"*Such a tragedy.*"

"*You said you had news,*" *said Mrs. Hamdy, pouring the tea and then remembering Gamal was still there.* "*Thank you, Gamal, that will be all.*"

He bowed to us and walked slowly toward the kitchen.

"*I located someone who was approached at the hotel by men working for Ayman two days after she disappeared. They asked this person if she knew where Rana was.*"

"Really?"

"Yes. The mind reels. I discovered that Rana left the hotel dressed in a burqa. Did she make her escape that evening and shepherd her parents to safety? Were your in-laws in good shape?"

"Oh, yes. Rahim played tennis and enjoyed sailing. His wife enjoyed walking the Gardens every day.'

I nodded. "Sailing?"

"Yes. He had a boat. He told us he sold it just before he disappeared. I think it was the day before he disappeared. Said he was getting too old."

There was much to process. I could see an escape plan now. A woman hiding in the anonymity of a veil, a boat supposedly sold or maybe actually sold or traded to procure another vessel, a Mediterranean departure in the dead of night to any of a thousand destinations.

No phones. No computers. No details in her manuscript beyond the fact that she had "a plan." Perhaps she had a bag of cash, gold, and jewelry; she had to have amassed a fortune in baubles over the years, and Rana knew from her charitable donations how easy it was to turn gems into cash.

Then, sitting there in Alexandria, turning all these possibilities over in my head, I realized another potential clue lay thousands of miles away…or, possibly, right here in Alexandria on my phone.

I thanked Mrs. Hamdy for the tea and the information and left.

As I searched for a cab on the street, a voice called from behind.

"Madame!"

It was Gamal.

"Madame. I overheard your remarks. You are a friend of Madame Rana?"

"Yes," I said, "I like to think that I am. But I never met her. I only know her through her writing."

"The Hamdy family is my family. They gave me a place to live. They sent my sons to school. I owe them everything."

"Yes. They seem like good people."

"First class, madame. First class. I worked for these people for many years. They are family to me."

"Do you have something to tell me, Gamal?"

He shook his head and turned around, looking to see if anyone was watching us. Satisfied, he began to nod, bobbing his head up and down,   grinning at me. For a moment I wondered if I was dealing with a madman. But he kept at it.

"No, madame. No. Nothing to tell you. Nothing." And as he continued nodding, he winked. Then he bowed, turned on his heels, and left.

This was a sign. A positive sign. I pulled out my phone, launched a browser, and punched a few words into the search box. I felt like an idiot. How had I only fixated on Rana? It was an honest mistake. I had read her book. I had thought about her mysterious identity. About her family and her vanishing trail. But I had ignored the other half of her beating heart, so to speak. The man she loved.

And there, on my small screen, was a picture of a handsome, brown-eyed, bearded man with a warm smile. And beside it, a head-line: Local Do-Gooder Vanishes in Europe.

Grant Hart was missing! He had disappeared. The article reported the longtime foreign aid worker had returned home to visit family in Shaker Heights, Ohio, after a long stint in Madagascar where he worked on increasing rice yields with local farmers. But after a week at home, he'd flown to Greece and had not been heard from since.

I pored over the article. His worried mother was quoted as saying, "Grant hugged me tight and told me it might be a while before he saw me again. He told me not to worry, but that's what mothers do. I pray he is safe and nothing bad has happened to him."

I stood there, the bright Mediterranean sunlight flooding down on me. All that had gone before was now illuminated. I knew I was done with this book of laughter, madness, fear, and love.

The precise details are lost. And yet I feel the evidence—a threat, a burqa, a search, a boat, a smiling servant, a missing American, a love—point to hope, to victory instead of defeat.

Somewhere, in my mind, at least, and I hope in yours, Rana Abboud and Grant Hart are safe together and in love. I see them on a Greek island or on the Turkish coast. And Rana's parents are nearby, too, in a neighboring fishing village, where Rana and her mother celebrate being fully alive, not fully compatible. Perhaps this vision is as deluded as the heroine we have spent so much time with, but I sense in my bones that this is not the case.

I pray one day that Rana Abboud will surface and conclude this book herself. But until that day, I'm thankful I can bring The Seductive Lady Vanessa of Manhattanshire *to a confident close, with an ending we all covet and deserve.*

An ending with love. An ending with bliss. An ending where, somewhere, Lady Vanessa and her creator are both enjoying the happiest of ever afters.

ABOUT THE AUTHOR

Seth Kaufman is a Brooklyn-based novelist and journalist. He has ghostwritten several nonfiction national bestsellers and is the co-author of the acclaimed exposé *Stealth War*. The *New York Times* called his book *The King of Pain* "one of 2012's most entertaining novels." His work has appeared in many national publications.